The Sound of Frost and Rain

霜雨集

王雅萍 著

丁海椒 译

上海文艺出版社
Shanghai Literature & Art Publishing House

图书在版编目（CIP）数据

霜雨集：汉英对照 / 王雅萍著；丁海椒译.

上海 ： 上海文艺出版社, 2024. -- ISBN 978-7-5321

-9092-8

Ⅰ. Ⅰ227

中国国家版本馆 CIP 数据核字第 2024NP0844 号

责任编辑：徐如麒　毛静彦
封面设计：孙豫苏
内页设计：兰伟琴
封面摄影：刘树昇

书　　名：霜雨集
作　　者：王雅萍著　丁海椒译
出　　版：上海世纪出版集团　上海文艺出版社出版
地　　址：上海市闵行区号景路 159 弄 A 座 2 楼　　201101
发　　行：上海文艺出版社发行中心发行
　　　　　上海市闵行区号景路 159 弄 A 座 2 楼　　www.ewen.co
印　　刷：常熟市东张印刷有限公司
开　　本：889×1194　　1/32
印　　张：9
字　　数：192 千字
印　　次：2024 年 9 月第 1 版　2024 年 9 月第 1 次印刷
书　　号：ISBN 978-7-5321-9092-8 /I.7152
定　　价：58.00 元

（敬启读者：如发现本书有印装质量问题，请与印刷公司联系　T：0512-52646971）

诗为序

丁海椒

秋天或有两种语言：
一个是雨，一个是霜。
装点她们的是满地的菊花，
奔放欢畅的金黄。

虽不是春日的五彩，
也不是夏天的光芒。
毕竟要启步走去深秋，
尚有红枫短暂的辉煌。

好在有大地慈祥的母亲，
容得下各种不同的声响。
她会将霜和雨全数收集，
去迎接来年必到的春光。

A poem as preface

Ding Haijiao

Autumn may have two languages.
One is rain, the other is frost.
Adorned with chrysanthemums all over the land,
Showing unrestrained and joyfully golden

Although not being spring's colorful,
Nor summer's strength and heat light.
After all, we are going off into late autumn,
Still have a short period of glorious red maple.

Fortunately, there is Earth kind mother,
Giving room for all kinds of sounds.
She will collect all the frost and rain,
To welcome the coming spring.

目 录

第二辑　山河之美
The beauty of mountains and rivers

第四辑　阅读之魅
The charm of Reading

第一辑 人生之思

The thoughts of life

幽暗中

时间像巨型的石磨，
将日子碾过。
岁月像无数的碎片，
积攒尘埃的遗落。
如太阳落入深山
幽暗陪伴着我，
人在寂寞中
倒也从容不迫。

Time Mill

Time is like a giant millstone,
Crushing the days into fragments.
As all the dust has been falling,
The darkness enveloped me.
I am feeling no lonely
but calm and leisurely.

梦醉时分

在梦与醒中穿行，
最是恍惚，
最是累赘。
多想抱着梦，
甜甜地息，
沉沉地睡；
多想将生活，
全都揉碎；
酿成美酒，
抑或蜜水；
流入梦里，
将心灌醉。

Make the dream drunk

Walking through dreams and wakefulness,

Most absentminded;

Most burdensome.

How I want to hold the dream,

To sleep soundly.

How I want to malaxate life,

To make the dream drunk.

收藏梦想

年近古稀
曾经想做的事情
已经力不从心，
曾经想看的书籍
也因为眼疾
只能悄悄收起。

恍惚间
事情与书籍
都已入梦境。
把一个个梦想
收藏起来
感觉她的气息。

.

Collect Dreams

When you're being old,

You're out of your depth.

You can't do what you want to do;

You can't read what you want to read.

They all went into the dreams.

But you have to know,

The dreams are worth collecting.

All the books and things you dreamed

Their smells are so fragrant,

So valuable and sweet.

希 冀

生活就在煎熬中
滴着它的雨声，
日子就在希冀中
弥漫它的风尘。

时间就在飞逝中
留下它的本能，
生命就在跌宕中
闪烁它的灵魂。

Hope

Life is suffering.

Tears are her raindrops.

Days living in hope.

Wind and dust are her prospects.

Time's flight,

Awakens her instinct;

Life's ups and downs,

Twinkles her soul.

我的影子

清晨的海滩
阳光下的影子
是那么修长
令我欢喜
也令我妒忌

真想钻进影子里，
让我做回影子，
那么气质
那么美丽
让我心旷神怡

晌午的草坪，
阳光下的影子，
竟像只大乌龟，
令我难堪
也令我惊异。

真想与影子分离，
让我做回自己。
影子却不理会，
只是慢慢爬行，
与我不离不弃。

阳光下，
一日的影子
并不如一；
一年中，
四季的影子
也并不如一。
但它却
始终如一
陪着你。

My Shadow

My Shadow on the beach in the morning,
Slim and slender, makes me jealous.
How I want to get into my shadow,
Keeping me young and pretty.

My Shadow on the lawn at noon,
Short and fat, a damn turtle.
How I want to rip my shadow,
Keeping the ugliness away.

My Shadow never cares what I think,
She's always with me, consistently.
Oh, how I want to kiss my shadow,
Keeping loyalty to myself.

一日之影
——译者和诗

我喜欢飞快地奔上清晨的海滩，
欣赏自己身影在初日下的修长；
青春美丽的你融进金黄的沙砾，
无尽的活力在海浪伴奏下释放。

但我实在不能拴住太阳的升起，
影子逐渐在脚下缩成龟壳一样；
午间的你承载我全部的责与重，
一步一印镌刻在前行的沙路上。

调皮的太阳终究把我丢进晚霞，
海滩上影子又变修长但稍迷茫；
感谢你在午间执着坚韧的刚强，
给了我黄昏里享受不尽的欢畅！

车窗里的影子

站在地铁
排着长队的入口
将来往的列车
静静等候。

随着列车进站
轻快的节奏
车窗的玻璃
飞闪着通透。

我的影子竟然
也在里面奔走
像与列车赛跑
我看着她晃悠。

我突然涌起
莫名的担忧
好像影子
有被碾压的征候。

瞬间，一阵惊喜
让我激情奔流
原来影子更早
与列车邂逅

我开始领悟
其奥秘的深厚
原来影子在演绎
我人生的漫游。

人生永远在路上
在漫漫旅途的
每一个站头
在闪亮的车窗后……

The Shadow in the Metro window

The train passed the Metro platform,
I saw my shadow in the window.
She was running so fast,
Like racing with the train.

I didn't feel torn apart or crushed,
But flowed with great passion.
My Shadow goes faster than I do,
Even passing the train ahead.

Suddenly it dawned on me,
Life is always on the road.
My destiny is to keep running forward
If only to carry my own shadow.

时间碎片

当时间被打成碎片
生活像散沙一般
思绪变得纷乱
诗句成了雨点。

我总是在恍惚间
惊恐地发现
时间像流星一般
将我抛得远远。

我总是梦中看见
时间像礼花一般
纷纷洒落
稍纵即逝地泯灭。

时间不再展现
它整体的威严
总是一地鸡毛
让人飘忽不安。

时间成了碎片
一切都在快闪
生活失去质感
哪有气定神闲。

时间成了碎片
思维难以连贯
唯有一片哀叹
诗意如浮云飘散。

Time became a fragment

Time could fall into pieces;
Time could fall into the sands;
Time could be a mess of hemp;
Time could be a useless raindrop.

Poetry is like floating clouds,
As long as you hold on to the fragment.
Time suddenly becomes a shooting star,
Pulsing light into the dark.

尝 试

我尝试将每一片光
装进记忆的收藏
我尝试用每一朵花
装点曾经的时光

我尝试让老照片
束上时代的封腰
我尝试让老日子
穿上最新的时装

回眸时见魔影魔幻
一切都在摇曳彷徨
飞奔而向真实天空
终于见到我的太阳

Try

I try to collect every beam of light,
Put into the cabinet of memory.
I try to use each flower,
Decorate all the past time.
I try to make the old photos,
Bundle on the waist tape of the era.
I try to make the old days,
Put on the most fashionable clothes.
I look back and see the full magic,
Everything is swaying and hesitating.
Finally, I fly up into the blue sky,
Try to find back my real sun again.

那年那场雪

当半个世纪的风
将时间剪成碎片
当半个世纪的雨
将岁月缝成褴褛

生活像沉重的鞋
走起来磕磕绊绊
日子却像那闪电
只觉弹指一挥间

碎片将黑发染白
褴褛将神态遮掩
却见那年那场雪
纷纷扬扬扑面来

The snow that I have met

Half a century of wind,
Cut time into pieces.
Half a century of rain,
Sew years into patchwork.

Life is like the heavy shoes,
Stumbling along the road.
The days passed like the lightning,
Just a flick of the finger.

Pieces of time dyed my hair white.
Rags hid my posture of old age.
But I saw the snows I have met,
Kindly coming at me.

月与雪

天上的月
地上的雪
伴着我度过
青春的岁月

月的圣洁
雪的纯洁
挡住狂飙
对灵魂的浩劫

心中的月
不为黑暗胆怯
心中的雪
与狂热决绝

梦中的月
伴我琼楼宫阙
梦中的雪
让我一起飞跃

The moon and snow

The moon is holy;
The snow is white.
They were my favorite when I was young;
My youth gushes out into holy white.

The bright white of the moon tells me,
"Don't be afraid of ugly darkness."
The pure white snow tells me,
"Don't get caught up in blinding fever."

Now the moon and the snow are still in my heart,
Admonish me pure to white and righteousness.
I would even have strange dreams
Of beautiful snowflakes falling on the moon.

四季雨雪

春雨淅淅沥沥
一脚水一脚泥
大地与我亲昵
踩下去拔不起

雷声滚过天际
夏雨如瀑而至
汗水雨水融一体
银锄闪电比靓丽

秋雨少有时机
却是透明的瑰丽
与金色相映成辉
与霜雪如胶似漆

冬雪是雨的结晶
北国风光最美丽
伐木的锯声凛冽
云裹着树梢坠地

Four seasons of rain

Falling the spring rain,
Mixes with earth into mud.
I could not pull my feet out,
Unwilling to give up the season.

Falling the summer rain,
Mixes with the sound of thunder.
Sweat and rain come together,
Race to see who is the most diligent

Falling the autumn rain,
Rare and precious.
Glistens with the color of gold.
We had a great harvest.

Falling the winter rain,
Turns into snowflakes.
The crystal of water,
The fruit of my whole year.

牵 手

和太阳牵手
走过炼钢炉口
此刻正窜出
熊熊的火头

和白云牵手
走过雪域大洲
圣洁的身心
在互致问候

和风儿牵手
走过春夏秋冬
那开心一刻
还在微微颤抖

和海浪牵手
一起随波逐流
紧紧依偎着
在天地间畅游

Hand in hand

Hand in hand with the Sun,
Through the opening of a steel furnace.
Coming out at that moment,
The flame, the color of life.

Hand in hand with white clouds,
Through the snowy continent.
Holy white body and mind,
Greetings to each other.

Holding hands with the wind,
Through spring, summer, winter and autumn
That happy moment,
Still trembling slightly.

Hand in hand with the sea waves,
Go with the flow together.
Close to each other,
Swimming between heaven and earth.

我见过你

在沙漠
我见过你
你是千年不倒
万年不朽的胡杨

在戈壁滩
我见过你
你在我绝望时
海市蜃楼模样

在雪夜
我见过你
燃烧的热吻
化开我冰裹的脸庞

在晨曦
我见过你
将一缕霞光
披在我的身上

你是我

冲破羁绊的梦想

你是我

天然生成的倔强

你是我

惺惺相惜的灵魂

你是我

生生不息的信仰

I've seen you

In the desolate desert,
I've seen you.
You're the immortal euphratica
Standing a thousand year.

In the Gobi Desert,
I've seen you.
When I'm in despair
A mirage becomes real.

On a snowy night,
I've seen you.
Your hot kiss in the frigid air,
Radiates through me.

In the early morning
I've seen you.
A ray of sunlight,
Suddenly put upon me.

In my whole life,

I've seen you.

No matter what difficulty encounter,

You are my faith and strength.

岁月的落叶

铁轨弯弯
像岁月弯弯的样子
岁月弯弯
像铁轨弯弯的样子

铁轨上
铺满了秋的落叶
层层叠叠
亦是岁月的落叶

一群大妈
站在铁轨上摆姿势
站得层层叠叠
她们挥手的瞬间
我忽地想起
就是当年站在火车上
与这座城市
告别的样子

原来这群大妈
也是岁月的落叶
我亦站上铁轨
做一片岁月的落叶

Fallen leaves

The Train tracks are curved,
Same as the curves of time.
The tracks have autumn leaf leaves on them,
They are the fallen leaves of the years.

Decades ago young girls boarded the train and left,
Now they are back looking for the track.
They are the fallen leaves of life,
But decorating the golden autumn.

Their dress is in bright colors,
Their various poses make people laugh.
They have worked hard all their lives,
Curve life track fills them with happiness.

春风的梦幻

岁月的风霜
雕琢斑驳的躯干
年轮的盘旋
铸起脊梁的身段

枯藤老树上
又见新枝与嫩芽
春风的梦幻
落入心中的柔软

The spring breeze

The spring breeze circled around the little tree:
Her trunk added a new annual ring.
The annual wheel carries whole year's dream,
Recording the tenderness of the spring.

Later the little becomes an old tree:
New shoots and dead branches always coexisting.
She never stops her new dream,
The new annual ring is waiting for spring.

心中的白桦林

梦中回到兴安岭
又见当年白桦林
半个世纪瞬间而过
彼此的心依然年轻

我第一次见到你
你的一身白衣
迷住了我的眼睛
虏获了我的心灵

推开山里的小屋
白雪皑皑无垠
你融于天地之间
让我欣喜亦震惊
我融于你的纯情
或许是人生之幸

当我第一次回眸
才见你乌黑眼睛

透过闪亮的窗棂
感觉你纯洁心灵

春天你露出嫩芽
让我欣然亲吻
丝丝气息入沁
夏时你枝繁叶茂
宛如绿色苍穹
为我挡雨遮阴
秋季你叶叶烁金
是我最美的书签
让阅读充满欢欣
冬日你扯下外衣
让我写封封情书
用眉目为我传情
最是温暖我的心

落叶一片一片
夹进书页
雪花一片一片
送走光阴
却送不走我的思念
我心中的白桦林

The birch forest in my heart

Dream of going back to the Hinggan Range,
See the birch forest at that year again.
Half a century has suddenly passed by,
Both hearts are still young.

The first time when I saw you,
You dressed all in white.
It caught my eyes,
And captured my heart.

Push cottage door opened in the mountain,
Boundless Snow lead me into Heaven and Earth.
Made me feel happy and shocked;
You were such an innocent blessing of life.

Spring, you let me kiss your tender leaves;
Summer, you sheltered me from the wind and rain;
Autumn, you gave beautiful leaves to mark my book;
Winter, you put holy white into my love letters.

Leaves one by one clip into the pages;
Snowflakes piece by piece send time away.
But can not send away my thoughts,
Of the birch forest in my heart.

雨中"七彩"

赤橙黄绿青蓝紫
却不是天上彩虹
更不是地上蘑菇
只是雨中的人
雨中的伞
组成了"七彩"
一起去做核酸

我是棵香樟树
只是在高处俯瞰
如此动人的美
让我忽闪着
婆娑的泪眼
我多想是一把
巨型的伞
为"七彩"们
将风雨遮拦

我望着对面

樱花的树冠
像苍穹一样
遮着云天
我羡慕他的伟岸
更羡慕他的洁白
那一树的花朵
像白衣天使一般

七彩透迤蜿蜒
像飘逸的彩带
并不是为摆拍
没有故意挑选
而是斑斓的色彩
在这里不期而遇
撑起了一个
特殊的春天

COVID-19 test in the rain

Red orange yellow green blue and purple
Not a rainbow in the high sky.
Just the umbrellas people hold in the rain,
Lined up for COVID-19 test.

A huge pattern made up,
Looks magical and unusual.
What exactly is she?
Answers kept pouring out from my heart.

Memorial to the deceased in the cabin hospital[1],
She is a large wreath.
Everyone's life is so precious,
Enough for the world to lament.

Thanks to the bravery of the medical staff,
She is a big medal.

---

1 The Cabin Hospital（方舱医院）is a temporary hospital which is constructed in emergency by using the original resources.

For the sake of public health
They risked their own lives.

To kill the virus completely,
She is a large encirclement.
This may not be the best approach,
But no move forward, no human expectation.

In my heart and in my dreams,
She is already gathered petals.
Spring has sounded the assembly call,
It shouldn't be too far away from us.

雨中"七彩"
——译者和诗

赤橙黄绿青紫蓝，
却不是彩虹挂在高天。
排队去做核酸检测
雨中人们撑起的小伞。

一个大大的图案组织起来，
看起来可真不是一般。
她到底是个什么？
我的心里不断涌出答案。

纪念方舱医院逝者
她是一个大大的花圈
每个生命都弥足珍贵
足够使全世界痛惋。

感谢医护人员的勇敢，
她是一个大大的奖盘。
为了公众的健康，

他们冒着生命的危险。

为了彻底追杀病毒，
她是一个大大的包围圈，
这办法也许不是最好，
但前行才能有人类的期盼。

在我的心里和梦中，
她是已经聚集的花瓣。
春天已经吹响了集结号，
离我们应该不会太远。

暴风雨中

风卷着雨
雨裹着风

一把把伞
似迎风绽开
像落花凋零

一蓬蓬发
被瞬间淋透
正滴水不停

一身身衣
已被撕烂
像逆风而行

一个个人影
穿透风雨
正砥砺前行

一种种搏击
以不屈的力量
展蓬勃的生命。

In the storm

In the heavy storm,
Trudging along with an umbrella.
The clothes got soaked through,
While I was in despair.

Suddenly I saw
Many are moving forward against the wind.
Then the umbrella felt stronger,
Hope is no longer lost.

The wind and rain will always pass.
Lives will not be finished.
I'd like to thank the storm,
For making me feel my own strength.

未来岛

随魔轮远航
去寻找未来岛
魔轮意外触礁
颠簸于万顷波涛

抢险堵洞救生
像泰坦尼克号
好在不是冰海
八仙各有妙招

船长稳坐钓鱼台
露出神秘微笑
我们撞上的
正是未来岛

The future island

Take a long voyage on a magic ship,
The destination is an island named Future.
The magic ship accidentally touched the reef,
Like the Titanic in a dangerous shipwreck.

All the crew were in a panic,
Only the captain smiled calmly,
What we hit is the very future island.
It's not an iceberg nor a rock.

There is plenty of food of all kinds;
There are fashionable clothes and daily utensils;
There are high-speed trains and highways;
There are even over 6G networks.

There are harmonious and peaceful social lives.
Of course there is no war, no disaster.
Everyone is working happily,
Enjoying the leisure time carefree.

Go ahead, Guys!

The captain called loudly.

When we want to give him a thank,

He is nowhere to be found.

外婆和我

外婆像弯弯的弓
我像离弦的箭
穿越漫漫的时间
回到幸福的童年

外婆像弯弯的月
我坐在上面撒欢
穿越茫茫的云层
满载新奇与浪漫

外婆像弯弯的船
我像摇橹的杆
穿越哗哗的流水
就在弹指一挥间

外婆像弯弯苍穹
我像升空的火箭
穿越浩渺的太空
拜访宇宙的神殿

Grandma and me

Grandma is like a curved bow;
I'm like an arrow shot out.
Through a long long time,
Back to the happy childhood.

Grandmother is like a curved moon;
I'm like a kid playing on it.
Through the vast clouds,
Full of novelty and romance.

Grandma is like a curved boat;
I'm like the paddle of the boat.
Through the rushing water,
Experiencing every moment.

Grandma is like a curved sky;
I'm like arising rocket.
Through the vast space,
Visiting the temple of the universe.

火星与星星

不要痴迷于
一粒火星的耀眼
毕竟它不是
天上星星的璀璨
稍纵即逝
是它的本性
只有星星
才有永恒的境界

一粒蹦跶的火星
就在我的眼前
一颗孤独的星星
挂在遥远的天边
火星或许只能
跳跃于瞬间
却喜欢它的炽烈
星星的寂寞
令人牵挂
当我仰望它时

便是星心相连

火星与星星
亦有手足情怀
只是一个在地
一个挂上了天

火星也可能燎原
星星亦可能塌陷
流星划过夜空而坠
火星忽闪几下而灭

带着诗意与梦幻
带着激情与期盼
都闪着明亮的眼
与我终身为伴

Mars and sparks

A planet of our sun named Mars^2,
And a bonfire both can make a lot of sparks.
But the sparks are not the Mars,
Even though they look the same sometimes.

Twinkle, twinkle, little star,
Sparkle, crackle little spark.
I wonder at a diamond in the sky,
Not the earth spark makes me shy.

2 Mars（火星）, in Chinese, literally means "The star of Fire."

今天也是我的六一

虽然已是银发熠熠，
却在那里寻寻觅觅，
捧出孩时的老照片，
坐上时光的穿梭机。

一个甲子瞬间穿越，
曾与孙子一样顽皮，
只是戴上了红领巾，
才有孙女一样笑靥。

我也曾是早晨太阳，
怎么瞬间落到山里？
时间犹如弹指一挥，
只见流星飞过天际。

礼花在夜空中绽开，
闪着老小孩的标记，
我像孩子欢呼雀起，
今天也是我的六一！

Celebrate the Children's Day[3]

Although sporting shining silver hair on my head,
I still look for something from time to time.
Oh, I'm looking for the young time,
Looking for my early black hair.

I was the rising sun in the morning,
How did I suddenly fall into the mountain?
Time is a speedy shuttle.
You can never catch it.

How I would like to build a new machine,
Which runs fast as the shuttle but in opposite direction.
Sitting on it, I will be back in grandkid's laughter,
To celebrate the International Children's Day.

---

3 June 1st is the International Children's Day.

我们的母校有多美

清晨，当第一缕阳光
透过母校的门楣，
你会感觉
母校的气质有多高贵。

黄昏，当一群小鸟
与枝头的绿波相随，
你会知道
我们的母校有多美！

百年神秘的白塔
隐在树隙间，
静静地静静地
令遐想放飞。

鹅绒般的大草坪
绿荫环抱，
放慢脚步
聆听细草低语入微。

荡漾的荷花池
古典柱上紫色瀑布，
虫鸣鸟啼
令人陶醉。

风雨操场　健身房
音乐教室　图书馆
曾经留下
嬉笑奔跑　读书声脆。

我们的豆蔻年华
有美的熏陶爱的伴随，
我们的学生时代
更加可爱更加纯粹。

教室里的阳光
温暖而明媚；
大礼堂的彩玻
浪漫而深邃。

母校有晨的朝晖
春的花蕾；
母校有夏的茂盛
冬的苍翠。

母校有秋天
浓浓的果味；
母校有园丁，
笑落的眼泪。

我们的母校
如此之美，
却在浩劫中
遭难受罪。

清澈的荷花池
顷刻被毁；
大礼堂的彩玻
全被砸碎。

我们的眼
盈满泪水；
我们的心
沉沉地下坠。

我们在迷茫中
离开母校的抚慰。
走向农村
走向边陲。

直到十年后
一声惊雷，
重返母校
才有了机会。

从此每年秋天
我们与母校约会，
金色的落叶
也让我们沉醉。

我们的校友
来自天南地北，
母校已万紫千红
满园芳菲。

光阴似箭
时间如飞，
半个世纪，
弹指一挥。

我们这一辈
渐显憔悴，
奋斗的人生
无怨无悔。

而我们的母校
则越来越柔美。
桃李的芬芳
沁入她的心扉。

前天
我们为母校骄傲；
昨天
我们为母校争辉；

今天
我们依然无愧；
明天
我们依然相会。

母校在我们眼中
总是熠熠生辉，
母校在我们心中
永远是那么美！

How beautiful our Alma mater is

Birds are perching on the branch at the school,
They kept singing without stop.
Wonderful, beautiful!
What a beauty our Alma mater is!

The lotus pond is still clear;
The auditorium still has color glass;
The classroom still is bright shining;
The goose-down lawn is still large and green.

Alumni from all over the world,
Whose successes started here at school.
All of them are dressed in bright clothes,
Decorating the school more colorful than ever.

红枫落叶

你鲜红欲滴
红得像一滴血
氤氲在叶上
你火红欲燃
红得像一团火
由内而外爆发

你却安静地
落在草丛上
将最后的美丽
装点荒芜的秋光
将尚存的暖意
扑进我的心房

我的眼在流泪
心却已腾起热浪
生命虽有尽头
灵魂依然芬芳
一片红叶故事
在我心中收藏

Red maple leaves

You are as red as a fire,

Outbreaking from the inside out.

You didn't burn yourself,

Quietly hiding in the grass;

To enrich next year's spring,

For the new flowers and shoots.

I looked at you without shedding tears,

But with a warm current in the heart.

Pop into my heart,

Your touching and sad story,

Store in my mind forever.

落叶书签

我将落叶夹进书里
让她生活在新天地
抚着她柔软的身姿
我感觉到她的呼吸
她将秋天带进书屋
氤氲着满满的诗意
她打开一扇扇窗户
透出我探寻的神秘

Bookmark

I put a fallen leaf into my book,
She makes the book feel fragrant.
She paints my study room with gold.
Then she thanks me in surprise:
"It was you who gave me a new space."

昨与今

你将昨日的倩影
投入今天的河里
让波纹忘记年龄

你将昨日的梦境
融入今天的心底
重叠消逝的光阴

你将昨日的忧郁
留在今天的眼底
揪住多少人的心

你将昨日的皱纹
化作今天的涟漪
将岁月沧桑染尽

Put yesterday in today

You put the young image of yesterday,
Fixed in the river of today,
Making the ripples forget their age.

You put the dream of yesterday,
Fixed to the mood of today,
Overlapping time passed.

You put the melancholy of yesterday,
Fixed to the eyes of today,
Holding on to so many hearts.

You put the wrinkles of yesterday,
Fixed to the face of today,
Wiping away the vicissitudes of time.

我的心

我把心搁在这里
你可以寻找到
我把情留在风里
你可以感觉到
我把昨日的心情打了包
你可以打开它
我把明天的期待投入邮箱
终究，你能收到

My heart to friends

I put my heart in the open;

You can find it.

I put my feeling in the wind;

You can share it.

I put yesterday's mood into the cabinet;

You can open it.

I put today's hope in mailbox;

Finally, you can receive it.

晚 霞

晚霞
蓄了一天的气韵
将自己绽放
晚年
蓄了一生的力量
将自己回放

朝霞是灿烂的
却带着青春的彷徨
午阳是热烈的
却带着炽烈的灼伤

晚霞是温和的
揉碎冰雪与风霜
晚年是祥和的
积淀岁月与沧桑

Sunset glow

Sunset glow stores the spirit of the whole day,
Blooming itself,
The sunset glow must surely be mild.

Old age stores the power of a lifetime,
Playing itself back,
The old age must surely be peaceful.

I like sunset glow
I enjoy old age time
Without turbulence, there is no steaming heat.

披在身上

将雪峰披在身上
便成了哈达
将国旗披在身上
便成了阳光
将战袍披在身上
便成了烈火
将月光披在身上
便进入梦乡

Put it over the shoulders

Put the snow peak over the shoulders,
It becomes hadaa[4].
Put the red flag over the shoulders,
It becomes sunshine.
Put the war robe over the shoulders,
It becomes a flame.
Put the moonlight over the shoulders,
It becomes a dream.

---

4 Hadaa (哈达) is a kind of silk fabric used by the people of Mongols and Tibet as a ritual.

岁月畅想

拟把岁月裁剪成礼花
绽放在历史的天空
拟把时间冶炼成钢花
铺设成人生的铁轨
拟把日子燃烧得纯青
提炼着生命的醇厚
拟将光阴折叠成金箔
闪烁着永恒的灵魂

Pamper imagination

Turn every second into a single grain,

Gather them into a pot of rice;

Turn every minute into a note,

Gather them into a piece of music.

Turn every hour into a whip,

Pushing me keep hard;

Turn every day into on a gold foil,

Giving out a dazzling light;

Turn each month into into fireworks,

Flashing with the spirit;

Turn each year into a steel rail,

Guiding forward,

Turn my whole life into a planet,

Orbiting the Solar System forever.

生日感怀

走在历史的隧道里
感觉岁月像一阵风
走在生命的轨道上
岁月便有山的沉重
吹生日蛋糕的烛光
岁月是悦耳的歌声
行走在日子的山谷
岁月是起伏的山峰
我想开着生命列车
让岁月的引擎自动
按着自然节奏前行
一切都在不经意中

Birthday

Birthday is a stop on the journey of life.

This day is to add water, refueling and charging.

The long journey has already sped by,

Future trips to dip into autonomous driving.

I don't like to step down on the brake,

Let my life move forward naturally.

时间的遐想

时间撑着
阳光的长杆
正划行在
岁月的长河
来不及欣赏
四季风景
小舟已匆匆
将年越过

人们倚着
生活的船舷
在奔涌的
激流中颠簸
来不及探究
潮起潮落
已被夕阳
挽住了胳膊

The reverie of time

Time holds up a long pole of sunshine.
It is the shadow in the long river of time.
Too late to enjoy the scenery of the seasons,
The boat has zipped through the whole year.

We lean on the boat side of life,
In the rushing jolt in the torrent;
Too late to explore the ebb and flow,
The setting sun held our arms warmly.

人生如烟

由一粒粒火星
坠入广袤人间
风吹起了火苗
是袅袅的炊烟

时而炙烤熏燎
气息郁闷浓烈
时而丝丝缕缕
阵阵清新恬淡

时而穿越风雨
跨过雷鸣闪电
时而飘逸悠然
出神入化境界

在辽阔的天际
飞出道风景线
让夕阳的余晖
融于云雾之间

Life is like smoke

Life is like a thick smoke,

Actually caused by little sparks one after another.

Sometimes through the wind and rain;

Sometimes across the thunder and lightning;

Sometimes elegant and leisurely;

Sometimes go to the realm of god.

I collect these sparks.

I compressed this smoke.

Put them in my poem,

And recite it when I have time.

天堂图书馆

到了这个年龄，
总会想到去天堂的事宜。
甚至有那么一些憧憬，
还有那么一丝惬意。

已经不止一次
听朋友说起，
天堂是一座图书馆，
那是最合我的心意。

天堂图书馆
是什么样式？
我纵情地展开
想象的羽翼。

云层是天然书架，
藏着海量的书籍。
云朵是轻柔的桌椅，
载着读者高高飞起。

仰望云层顶端，
雪藏镇馆的典籍。
若想借阅赏析，
请上登顶云梯。

这个场景多么震撼
又多么熟悉，
它让我想起
登顶珠峰的人梯，

那是由人的
血肉之躯架起，
我曾为他们
惊极而泣……

电子阅览室
更有些诡异，
蓄电池的能量
由闪电供给。

但它却链接起
每一个星际，
宇宙文明的浪花
顿时在眼前涌起。

我竟然看到了
走出白桦林的足迹，
还有雪地上
飞奔的爬犁。

我竟然找到了
海派文化的源流，
一代宗师的画作
在天地间飘逸。

那种温馨的感觉
让我泪如雨滴，
钟馗的脸上
也挂满了笑意……

我问阳光借支笔，
想登天梯借书籍。
天使摁下遥控器，
天书落入手心里。

再不用担心身体，
再不用顾及眼疾，
像海绵落入天河里，
我如渴似饥。

天堂图书馆
如海洋般大气。
在那里阅读
领略无比神秘。

只需摁动按钮，
不用费尽眼力，
一目十行而过
全都融入我心里。

这样的图书馆，
让我心旷神怡，
那是滋养灵魂
最终的意义。

Paradise library

At this age, I always think about going to heaven.
A friend said, Paradise is a library.
I imagine what the Paradise library looks like.
The more I think, the more excited I become.

The air forms the natural bookshelf;
The clouds forms table and chair;
The battery is powered by lightning;
Angels press the remote control.

Mount Everest is a ladder;
Climb up on it and you can read books of life.
I saw all the books of my life were collected;
No single one was lost nor contaminated.

There were my youth photos in the birch forest;
There were my footprints in Shanghai metropolis;
There were my water drops in Shanghai style culture;
There were my love and friendship everywhere.

I can't help getting drunk reading these books.

An angel told me I wasn't allowed to read any more.

I replied kindly and with a smile:

I read it to be able to add a few copies.

第二辑 山河之美

The beauty of mountains and rivers

烟雨廊桥[5]

雾蒙蒙，
　　雨飘飘，
休闲地漫步
在枫泾廊桥。

迷迷蒙蒙的雨，
斑斑驳驳的桥，
一样的景致，
别样的风貌。

河面横跨着
古朴的廊桥，
河岸蜿蜒着
同样的美妙。

5　上海枫泾古镇有一长廊，全长268米。长廊里侧，是商店和民房，外侧是一条小河，与上海市中心以及浙江、江苏等地相通。相邻的千灯镇是历史文化遗产昆曲的发祥地。

多少遗梦
渐渐缥缈，
悠悠长廊
漫漫缭绕。

举目仰望
飞檐的木雕，
俯身凝视
倒影的妖娆。

咖啡座飘逸着
浪漫的情调，
恍惚中走过来
美丽的阿娇。

Fengjing[6] *long Bridge*

It's not the bridges of Madison County,
I am walking in Fengjing.
In the fog, in the rain,
Viewing the spot-peeled gallery.

The wood carvings of the cornices,
The enchanting reflection.
How many old dreams,
Gradually dim.

Cafe is flowing romantic sentiment,
The riverbanks were winding the same wonder.
Walking along in a trance,
I meet beautiful girl Ajiao.

---

6 Fengjing (枫泾), a typical ancient water town in Jingshan, Shanghai.

双 桥[7]

大画家的杰作[8]，
将她推上了星座。
双桥像把钥匙，
解开历史之锁。
那是深深的思念，
浅浅的碧波。
那是浓浓的乡愁，
淡淡的笔墨。
勾起一汪绿波，
激荡人的心窝。

---

7 周庄双桥，世德和永安两桥位于江苏省周庄中心，建于明代，两桥相连，像古代的钥匙，又称钥匙桥。著名画家陈逸飞的油画《故乡的回忆》使之闻名。

8 指的是陈逸飞1984年回到故乡，创作的油画《故乡的回忆——双桥》。美国石油大王哈默购下此画，作为礼物，赠给中国领导人邓小平。

Twin Bridges[9]

The Twin Bridges built in the Ming dynasty
Designed in the shape of an old key.
Why did they leave the key for posterity?
So young generations could step into their hearts?

Stepping into someone's heart is a hard thing.
Not to mention these people lived hundreds of years ago.
No wonder we want to and can't,
But we hold the key and never give up.

Not until it becomes a masterpiece of a great painter,
Does the the hometown of the heart reveal a little bit of secret.
Then the Twin Bridges became a superstar,
Always brings up the green waves in people's hearts.

---

9 Twin Bridges（双桥）, located in Zhouzhuang, Jiangsu province.

三　桥[10]

是一幅自然画作，
也将人的心撩拨。
桥在纵横间洞开，
船在桥洞中穿梭。
岸上枯老的树木，
沉积着岁月的蹉跎，
河边古朴的灯笼，
折射着时光的交错。

10　上海金山区枫泾三桥，由清风桥、竹行桥、北丰桥组成，三桥相连，组成难得优美的风景。

Triple Bridge[11]

A painting of nature,

Brings joy to the people's heart.

The bridge opens in both vertical and horizontal lines.

The boat shuttles through the archway.

The old trees on the shore,

Precipitated by centuries of time.

Quaint red lantern by the river,

Reacting to the staggered time.

How I want to build the fourth bridge!

Surround it with all the beautiful scenery.

Or ancient, or modern,

Link the glories of the five continents.

---

11 Triple Bridge（三桥）, located in Fengjing, Shanghai.

长廊与绿波[12]

河岸的风雨廊

悠长悠长

河里的绿波

蜿蜒远方

都是一眼

望不到尽头

像人生一样

漫长而迷茫

曾走过多少

这样的长廊

曾见过多少

这样的波浪

而人生的路

可遇不可求

---

12 这个风景在江苏省昆山市锦溪镇，东临淀山湖，西依澄湖。有十眼长廊桥，下面绿浪翻腾。

机遇和命运
在一起飞翔

落入长廊的
初恋的幽会
落入绿波的
腾起细的浪
走过长廊
又一番景象
越过绿波
已见着夕阳

The corridor and green wave[13]

The corridor is a life with no end in sight;

Green wave is a time without any surprise;

A strange scenery was that in the water town.

The sweetness of the first love was in the corridor,

A worry-free childhood raced through the green wave.

I didn't want to walk through this long corridor,

And didn't want to leave that green wave.

But this is the only way out not for me to choose.

Or go to the the neighboring town Qiandeng,

Its thousand lights for the stages of life

Explain the joys and sorrows of life.

Then returning to the corridor and green wave,

Gives everyone a huge surprise.

---

13 This landscape is in Jinxi, Kunshan, Jiangsu province.

彩虹桥[14]

走过漫漫长桥
有跨海的味道
那么悠长悠长
如履时光隧道

倚着桥栏拍照
背景依然是
蜿蜒的桥
无数桥洞相连
像无数展翅的鸟

当你回眸远眺
一条彩虹湖面飘
与波涛热切亲吻
仙子下凡的妖娆

14　上海淀山湖建设了一座长达1470米的彩虹桥，既有现代桥梁的宽阔大气，又有传统石拱桥的古朴优雅，目前是长三角地区最长的拱桥。

Rainbow Bridge[15]

Walk through the long, long bridge,

Go through the ocean, or go through the state?

Like passing through a time tunnel,

A rainbow crosses the banks of the lake.

The birds are resting up there,

Kissing the calm water,

Thinking they were sky fairies.

---

15 The Rainbow Bridge（彩虹桥）is built on the Dianshan Lake.

母亲河

清晨我走过母亲河
雾霾笼罩着她的前额
我看不清她明亮的眼
却闻得她细声的护呵

午间我走过母亲河
阳光似炙烤般灼热
百年不遇的酷暑啊
江河湖海都觉干渴

深夜我走过母亲河
月光照着她苍白脸色
日夜奔忙留下的皱纹
恰是晚风吹起的微波

The Mother River

Early morning I walked across Mother River,
The haze shrouded her forehead.
I couldn't see her bright eye,
But could smell her soft care.

High noon I walked across Mother River,
The sun brought scorching heat.
The hottest summer in a hundred years,
All rivers and lakes feel thirsty and parched.

Late night I walked across Mother River,
The moon shone on her pale face.
The wrinkles left by the rush of the day and night,
Were the tiny waves of the evening breeze.

小河如镜

走上小桥
见河面出奇平静
眼前闪过
梳妆台前一面镜

抬头仰望
云姑娘妩媚弄影
扭头一看
秋姑娘正摆造型

原来她们
全都以小河为镜
浓妆淡抹
才有迷人的秋景

The river is like a mirror

Ascending the stone arch bridge,

The river below surprisingly calm,

Like standing in front of the dresser mirror.

The cloud girl shows a charming smile;

The autumn girl strikes an open pose.

I take pictures one after another,

To remember the magnificent autumn scenery.

乘 船

岸边的白墙黛瓦
微波正涂鸦油画
船娘悠悠地摇橹
搅动起一池水花

小桥似彩虹横跨
倒影将桥拽河下
小舟向圆洞而去
如入仙境的佳话

Boat

They all with the river as the mirror,

So that had a charming autumn scenery.

But the secret was more than that,

The white walls and black tiled on the shore.

River waves were painted with oil,

The boat woman rowed long.

Stired up a pool of water flowers,

The stone bridge a rainbow.

Boys mysteriously pass through the bridge arch,

Keeping a date with a wonderland fairy.

秋风写意

秋风挥着笔
大胆地写意
多情是她的灵气
所有的色彩
都在她笔下
点缀着大地
无情是她的收笔
所有的色彩
都让她泼尽
只留下白雪熠熠

The autumn wind painting

The autumn wind waved her brush,

Painting with amazing courage.

Love was her inspiration,

Dressing up the earth as colorful.

Jealousy was her failure,

Finally giving the world a monochrome look:

Leaving only the shining snow.

秋如画家

秋风是最好画家
她一挥洒
五彩便上了树
赤橙黄绿紫
像绽开的礼花
她一豪放
五彩便纷纷扬扬
在天地间飞卷
无限的遐想
当五彩落定
大地便悉心收藏
留下她最美的画

The best autumn painter

The autumn wind is the best painter.

She waves her brush once,

All the colors immediately reach the tree.

She waves her brush twice,

The colors fall quietly on the ground.

The earth carefully collects them,

Showing the most beautiful painting.

秋 景

秋天将阳光披身上
让你赏一树树金黄
像时光秀那么耀眼
在天地间纵情奔放

秋天将火焰挂枝上
尽燃了春夏的辉煌
片片枫叶如血欲滴
恰似那火红的夕阳

秋天将星星藏心上
裹紧风衣独自惆怅
当她敞开胸怀之时
竟是漫天雪花飞扬

Autumnal scenery

The most willing to give you golden is autumn,
Joy of the harvest all the way;
The most hope to give you red is autumn,
Full maple leaves call from the mountain;
The most likely to give you blue is autumn,
Naive color covers all the sky;
The most mysterious giver of white is autumn,
Telling you about true nature.

赏昙花

你在仲夏之夜
静静地开放
我以秒来计算
你最美的时光。

仙人掌的血脉
在你身上流淌
迷人的气息
氤氲你的芬芳。

你的花瓣
像月光皎洁
你的花蕊
像灯丝闪亮。

你是天上仙子
像飘逸的雪花
你是月下美人
那玲珑的模样。

你瞬间的精彩
如相机的曝光
将永恒的靓丽
留在人的心上。

Enjoy queen of the night flower[16]

On a midsummer's night,
You would be in full bloom for an instant.
The most exciting time,
Can only be calculated in seconds.

The blood of the cactus
Flows through your body.
The royal fragrance
Elegant but dense.

You are a fairy in heaven;
You are the beauty of the moon.
The good moments will last forever,
At least in my heart.

---

16 Queen of the night flower（昙花）, epiphyllum.

2429228

一束鲜花

一束鲜花静静绽放
玫瑰好像特别矜持
将外衣裹得紧紧
不让偷窥心的秘密

百合开得特别豪爽
毫无顾忌敞开胸襟
让心中的一丝一缕
都在你眼前闪熠

花蕊像满天的星星
护着身边羞花闭月
我这才恍然明白
这最美的姐妹情谊

A bunch of flowers

A bunch of flowers blooms quietly;
The rose seemingly reserved.
Wraps her coat up tightly,
Protecting her secrets from peepers.

The lily is open and generous,
Opens her mind with no scruples;
Shows all wisps in the heart,
Goes straight into your eyes.

The various flower buds are guards,
Around them closely.
Then I figure it out:
They are two sisters.

风信子

家里多了一盆花
从大蒜头窜出身架
绿得那么鲜嫩
像一座玲珑小塔
绿珠儿一颗颗泛红
色彩是动心的高雅
玫红的珠儿绽放
像美女头上的卷发
才见长长的茎挺拔
有了亭亭玉立模样
水仙般的叶像裙摆
衬着百态娇媚的花
几度猜测她的名字
方知她是远渡重洋

Hyacinthus

Another potted flower at my home,

Who knew she was from the Mediterranean?

The flower buds is like curls on a pretty girl's head,

The petals, the most fashionable skirt.

The tall stem,a slender leg.

The drops of water on her are like charming tears.

Who could write down her name,

In the language of the Flower God in the Louvre?

初见木槿

她有点像虞美人
亭亭玉立的范儿
却不那么孤傲
她更喜欢抱团

她有点像粉蝴蝶
在风中漫舞飞闪
却不是蜻蜓点水
愿守一方的灿烂

一堵堵的花墙
一片片的花海
一簇簇的花丛
一座座的花巅

奔走于她的河谷
徜徉于她的微澜
藏匿于她的密丛
依偎于她的胸怀

享受她的美与爱
在每个心动瞬间
穿着古装的美女
与她携手向未来

First saw hibiscus

She is a bit like a poppy, [17]
A graceful style but but never alone.
She is a bit like a pink butterfly,
Dancing brightly in the wind.

Running in her river valley,
Hidden in her dense cluster.
Beautiful woman of an old fashion,
Join hands with her to brace the future.

---

17 Papaverrhoeas, 虞美人。Papaver rhoeas, with common names including common poppy, corn poppy, corn rose, field poppy, Flanders poppy, and red poppy, is an annual herbaceous species of flowering plant in the poppy family Papaveraceae.

赏 花

一个花季的姑娘
走在樱花树下
一身和服
在她衣架般身上
飘出异域风尚
一双木屐
在与木栈道击掌

树上的花儿
摆着各种姿态
与她相望
不知她在赏花
还是花在赏她
调皮的几朵
跳上她的头
点缀她的发
挂在她的耳边
映着她的脸颊

靓丽的花枝
垂在她的额头
姑娘闭起了眼
闻着花朵的芬芳
如痴如醉的模样

满树的樱花
盘在她的头上
如女王的皇冠
缀满的不是珠宝
而是一片春光

Enjoy the cherry blossom

She wore a kimono printed with cherry blossoms,
Thick wooden clogs on her feet.
Walk forward along the cherry-tree path,
On the boardwalk with "pa-pa" sound.

She looked at the cherry blossoms,
People also looked at her clothes.
She didn't know other eyes were looking at her,
Seeing a kind of exotic fashion and tune.

She had a smile on her face.
People laughed at her.
She didn't know the laughter came for her,
Showing a kind of exotic ridicule.

古 园

一座花园

尽染古朴的气息

一堵围墙

环绕千年的陈迹

一组顽石

尝试越墙的姿势

一行杉木

亲吻羞涩的云霓

Garden in old time

A garden was breathing smells of the old days
A wall was having traces around thousands of years
A set of stone was trying to move over the wall
A line of fir was kissing the shy cloud

雨 珠

雨一滴
一滴地下着
很精心的样子
荷叶上
雨珠蹦跶着
很欢快的样子
花瓣上
雨珠镶嵌着
很璀璨的样子
小草上
雨珠黏贴着
很温馨的样子
屋檐上
雨珠倒挂着
很调皮的样子

Raindrop

The rain fell drop by drop,

Carefully and carefully.

Drop on a lotus leaf,

Bouncing around with cheer;

Drop on a flower Petal,

Embedding in her bright shape;

Drop on a little grass

Clinging to her gentleness and fragrance;

Drop on the eaves,

Only showing her naughtiness.

石库门

百年的石库门
又焕发了青春
岁月带着容光
让她分外精神

漆黑的大门
紧闭着当年遗风
闪亮的门环
荡漾着耳垂光晕

旗袍女踩着高跟
重现着优雅神韵
月光穿过屋檐
跟上她的脚步声

Shikumen[18]

Shikumen combines European and Chinese styles.

The dark door closed so many legacy,

Once opened, blows the wind of a hundred years,

Shining door ring shows halation of old French Concession.

The cheongsam woman stepped on high heels,

And now she wears stylish low-cut clothes.

The door plate marks the aspiration of generations,

Are now on the road of thriving and prosperity.

---

18 Shikumen（石库门,The literal meaning is Stone Warehouse Gate）, is a kind of building in Shanghai.

时尚街

一条街将两边坐拥
如左搂右抱着女神
一位像阳光般热烈
一位像月光般清冷

左边让人摄魄钩魂
街心涌动着荷尔蒙
一对老外步履匆匆
追逐他们的巴黎梦

摇晃着殷红的酒杯
在梦境里谈笑风生
迈进DIRO的世界
疑似彩蝶飞入花丛

右边幽暗的石库门
屋里的灯光探出身
与静谧月光打招呼
也是悄悄细细的声

更令人诧异是壁画
勾勒出年代的灵魂
老建筑的每个部件
在时尚光影里重生

Fashion street

An odd street has two sides,

Like holding the goddess from left to right.

The right side seems filled with lights and fashion:

There comes belly-exposed girls and their boyfriends.

McDonald's and Starbucks are no longer new,

French Lafite and English whiskey are their favorite.

Some of them speak foreign languages,

Skillfully use knives and forks to eat steak.

The left side seems to be dim and out-of-date:

Noodles and dumpling are well sold.

There comes foreign friends from around the world,

No problem to use chopsticks but not skillfully.

Yangzhou fried rice is their favorite staple food;

Large pieces of Braised pork is their must-ordered dish.

They can't speak too much Chinese yet,

But enough to communicate with the waiter.

The goddess is looking at the two street sides with mirth,

Sprinkled divine water to both sides no stingy.

边 城

大家笔下的边城
是我心中的梦
摄友镜头的边城
闪着时尚的韵

晨曦里的边城
自然秀美迷蒙
恍若是翠翠
述说今世前生

灯光里的边城
璀璨夺目诱人
仿佛横空出世
诞生的水晶宫

岸上蜿蜒着边城
水中荡漾着边城
在人们的眼里
她是一颗星辰

The remote city

The remote city described by a master,
Was living in my dream;
The remote city photographed by a master,
Was the rhythm in my heart.

The remote city in the dawn,
Beautiful and misty as nature.
The remote city in the light,
As a Crystal Palace giving birth.

The wind blew over her on the shore,
Rippled her in the water.
In all people's eyes,
She is really a diamond.

山里的雾

雾，在山里
就像是一团谜
不知从天上飘来
还是从地下升起
迷迷蒙蒙的幻觉
清清沥沥的水汽
那是山在呼吸
林在透气
一半的清醒
一半的醉意

雾，在山腰
就像云在漂移
缭绕在我脚下
掩隐整个谷底
飘飘逸逸的仙境
恍恍惚惚的梦呓
那是天然之作
才具这样魅力
一半是景致
一半是虚拟

The fog in the mountains

Fog in the mountains is a mystery.
Where does it come from?
From the sky or from the earth?
Its arrival brings illusion.

I'd rather keep this illusion,
Keep me half sober, half drunk.
Feeling the forest breathe,
The spring water dance.

云中岛

云雾遮天蔽日
有一块裸露地
便成了云中岛
依然很有气势

周边茫茫的白
岛中层层的绿
更像云海母亲
孕育自己的孩

风在微微地吹
雾在渐渐地散
只等云开日出
大自然的分娩

An island in the cloud

Clouds and mist cover the sky and sun,
An island in the sea of cloud appears.
Is it Mother Earth breeding her child?
Or the dragon father caressing its belly?

The wind was blowing slightly,
The clouds gradually left.
Then see a high mountain peak,
The island turned out to be his proud head.

五言《云中岛》
——译者和诗

云海露一岛，
疑似妊娠早。
待到日出时，
奇峰傲顶俏。

屋脊与山脊

眼前是一幢幢屋脊
远眺是一座座山脊
屋脊是人工的造诣
山脊是天公的神迹

人工竟然那么细腻
片片鱼鳞般的瓦砾
层层叠叠错落有致
胜过了绣女的手艺

天公总是那么大气
挥起他的如椽大笔
牵着江河东奔西走
连起群岭壮观逶迤

屋脊为人遮风挡雨
山脊为天承受霹雳
一样的超凡脱俗
一样的心旷神怡

House roofs and mountain ridges

Before me were the house roofs,

In the distance were the mountain ridges.

The house roofs were artificial,

Delicate and clever.

The mountain ridges came from the nature,

Spectacular and meandering.

The house roofs were the shelter of the people;

The mountain ridges bears the thunderbolt for the sky;

So they are the same in my heart.

夕阳下的珠峰[19]

古老的夕阳

抚着年轻的珠峰

眼里放着温柔的光

妩媚的云朵

绕着雄壮的珠峰

心里做着甜蜜的梦

珠峰甩开了云朵

让她像丝带一样

飘然而去

珠峰伫立在夕阳下

像思考者的模样

他撑起的天空

让夕阳更加辉煌

---

19 此诗（中文）发表在《上海外滩》2022 年第 10 期。

Mount Everest

The setting sun of very ancient times,
Touching the youngish Mount Everest.
The setting sun shone his height;
The birds never reach his head.
The charming clouds with whiteness,
Like to surround and cuddle him.
He connects them with ice and snow,
Having a sweet dream in his heart.
But he pretends to be a cool model:
The thinker sculpture of Auguste Rodin.

悬崖上的家

你的家在山里
一面临大海
一面是峭壁
你的家在山里
炊烟与云霞相拥
灯光与星光相依
是天上还是人间
神奇旖旎迷离

Your home

Your home is on the cliff,

Cooking smoke curls up among the clouds;

Your home is facing the sea,

The lamp lights hidden among the stars.

Is it heaven or earth?

Magic charms blurred.

长江第一湾[20]

绿宝石的水面
金黄色的沙滩
深褐色的群山
草红花的镶嵌。

一道道色彩相间
一层层惊艳铺展
一圈圈碧波环绕
一片片金滩耀眼。

大自然的调色盘
美丽得让人心颤
千古风韵集一身
要数长江第一湾。

---

20 此诗（中文）发表在《上海外滩》2022 年第 10 期。

The first turn of Yangtze River

The surface of the emerald,
Set in golden sand beach.
Dark brown jade mountains;
A Mosaic of red grass flowers.

The Yangtze River flows through here;
This is her first turn.
Thus she becomes so beautiful,
All her way to Shanghai

七言《长江第一湾》
——译者和诗

红花绿珠黛玉山，
迎来长江第一湾。
从此扬子变靓女，
一路美到上海滩。

瀑 布[21]

你曾是一条小溪
蜿蜒在山里
流经高峡平湖
与江河融为一体。

你总是那么调皮
喜欢嬉戏
那天路过悬崖
你只身跃入谷底。

这一跳还真炫目
飞流直下千百米
这一跳改变命运
从此挂上了峭壁。

像舞台的幕布
随着日光开启

---

21 此诗（中文）发表在《上海外滩》2022 年第 10 期。

你的倾情演出
让多少人心悸。

你不再温柔静谧
吼出了你的声息
有排山倒海之势
有雷霆万钧之力。

你成了神话传奇
众人被惊得嘘唏
蜂拥而至的欢喜
在瞬间风靡大地。

Waterfall

You were once a small stream,

Winding in the mountains.

You are always so naughty,

Unwilling to merge into a flat lake.

You passed the cliff as you took,

A thrilling jump to the valley bottom,

Dropping a hundred meters with a splash.

Then you became a beautiful picture,

Suspended in nature and in people's hearts.

晨曦中的瓦村[22]

晨曦投下的色彩
是黑夜未退的蓝
一道道篱笆的黑
撑着雪地的白。

一缕阳光打翻
上帝的调色盘
五彩洒落瓦村
满眼尽是斑斓。

绿中透蓝的湖面
庄稼比阳光灿烂
金黄橙红深褐色
斑驳陆离的深浅。

岸边风景更惊艳
丽水拨弄倒影脸
如花似玉般装点
山神为之动心弦。

---

22 此诗（中文）发表在《上海外滩》2022 年第 10 期。

A village in the morning light

By the light of the early morning sun,

A village of tiled houses shows color.

The night faded away gradually,

So the blue of the walls turned brighter and brighter.

The cooking smoke was curling up,

So the brick red flashes like sparks.

There is a mist on the lake,

So the emergence of green was even more shy.

The mountains are full of azaleas,

So the purple came out of the young leaves.

The fields are covered with ears of wheat,

So the golden yellow is brighter than the sun.

This is nature's pigment palette,

More wonderful than the most brilliant painting.

孤　独

月亮孤零零地挂天边
没有云彩作伴
星星凄清地照在山间
没有灯火阑珊

小路径直地横在山里
没有岔道相连
孤独像浓雾散开
已经漫过我的心尖

loneliness

The loneliness of the moon,
Was hanging far away from the horizon.
No clouds in the sky,
Around her to accompany her.

The loneliness of the star
Was the bleak light in the sky
No single lamp to contrast with,
The earth was all but dark

The loneliness of the pathway,
Was going straight across the field.
No fork ahead,
Let her whirled round.

The loneliness of the girl,
Is the sweetheart ignored.
No one knows her thoughts,
Nor gives her a little warmth.

The loneliness of myself,

Was a sudden loss of thought.

With no direction of effort,

Every day lived only to steal leisure.

孤 独
——译者和诗

星星的孤独
是凄清地照在天间
没有一盏灯光相映
大地上一片黑暗

小路的孤独
是径直地横在田野
没有一个岔道
来给它回旋

姑娘的孤独
是心上人不理不睬
没有人知晓她的思念
给她一点温暖

自己的孤独
是突然丢失了意念
没有了努力的方向
一天天只有偷闲

观胡杨林

若与死神比肩
怀疑自己的灵魂
已经走远
若与胡杨比肩
我不知他究竟
带我去了远古
还是去了未来

只见他的身形
已褪去锦绣衣衫
青面獠牙的枯木
露着僵尸的怪诞

骷髅的鸟儿
衔着橄榄枝
调皮的孩儿
在她的腰间
顺势滑下来

现代人梦想瞬移
好像机器人大赛
而胡杨占领高地
傲然屹立数千年

Populus euphratica forest

If you were with the God of death,
You would have doubted your own soul;
If you were with populus euphratica,
You would have doubted your place.
They lived in ancient times,
And will still live in the future.
If there had been a little water supply,
The results would have been different.
Life goes on and endures in history,
Compete with AI computers and robots.

荒 芜

枯黄的草
编织着袋子
将冰冷的土地
装进她的怀里

一马平川的草坪
此刻有些孤寂
起伏的坑洼里
有落叶的聚集
更像小河微澜
旋起的涟漪

仰头望见
光秃秃的树枝
是一棵棵银杏
那金灿灿的落叶
曾让多少人痴迷
这是曾经的殿堂
居然也斑驳陆离

抽干落叶的精气
此刻这里已
成为他们的遗迹
心里涌起悲哀
眼前却是荒芜
我何尝不是叶子
终将化作春泥

Waste grassland

I stood by a wasteland,
It was once lined with trees:
Where the flowers are all in bloom.
Now the leaves of the Golden Gingko are gone.
The lawn cries in the potholes.

Desertification must be a force of nature;
Waste is human behavior.
Going out of cultivation is the waste,
Not consistent with human civilization.

I'm also sad,
But I never cry.
I want to turn into spring mud and
Cultivate the next year's scenery.

上海之鱼[23]

"上海之鱼"
没有经典故事
没有特别景致
仅以一个概念
就在那里风靡

"上海之鱼"
从空中俯瞰
无人机摄下的
岛屿有些迷离
她的形象堪比
一条腾跃的鱼

鱼的灵气源自
国际大师的设计
迪拜的棕榈岛

---

23 上海之鱼又名"金海湖",是上海奉贤新城的核心景观湖,占地8.74平方公里,系上海湖面面积第三大的人工湖。

亦是他的神笔
此刻又挥出奇迹

鱼鳍鱼身鱼尾
在湖面波光熠熠
让人心旷神怡
一个创意带起
一片崭新的天地

Shanghai Fish Park

People who have been to Palm Island in Dubai,

Come to the Shanghai Fish Park Today.

Clean up the picnic basket,

Set up the tour line.

Come to the bank of Jinhai Lake：

Once a small fishing village now Shanghai Fish Park,

With fish fins, fish body, fish tail - three parts.

Making you smelled the umami of the fish,

With a small "annual harvest" garden:

Wishing your income more than enough every year,

Give you a bunch of magnolia flowers.

You will no longer envy Palm Island, Dubai.

第三辑　天地之谜

The Mystery of Heaven and earth

淡淡的阳光

淡淡的阳光
淡淡的雾气
都懒洋洋的
伸展着

忽的，阳光
露出矛的本性
比箭更快疾
比剑更锋利

阳光雾霾搏击
从来扑朔迷离
只是一个转身
已经风和日丽。

Sunshine

The sunshine is sometimes faint,
Sometimes suddenly very fierce,
Touches you gently when she is faint,
Pricks you with countless needles when fierce.

The light mist is like a curtain,
Between the faint and fierce of sunshine.
When the sunshine is as sharp as a spear,
She protects you from the stabbing.

I will make a curtain rope,
Collect and control the mist:
Only a little bit open in the summer,
Wide open in the winter.

去太阳里躲一躲

这个春天，
时冷时暖，
乍暖还寒。
真想逃离，
抑或私奔。
去太阳里躲一躲，
伸个懒腰，
抑或舒展全身。
哪怕变成灰烬，
变成滚滚红尘。
随着暖风
慢慢升腾。

Hide inside the sun

To elope in the early spring,

When it becomes warmer but is still chilly,

Hide inside the high Sun,

Stretch a little then the whole body.

Even if it burns me into ashes,

I'll turn into the warm wind and rise slowly.

尘 埃

你是一颗尘埃
在我眼前轻轻飘落
我不知你飘向何处
没想过你是否有窝

阳光里我看你飞舞
脸上还带着笑涡
那劲头比街舞疯狂
你的指尖将光影划破

你落在我头上脸上
在哪里都可以做窝
我忍不住赶你走
你从缝隙悄悄钻过

我何尝不是尘埃
羞愧缠绕着心窝
只不过我缠着地球
你却偷偷缠住了我

The dust

A speck of dust comes quietly to me,
It has no luster, no glory.
No one knows where it came from,
Nor knows where it is going,
Nor Even how long it will stay.
No one cares, except for me.

Dust is one of the smallest items;
It flies all its life until its head grays.
All the time it changes its way.
Everywhere is its destiny.
Few people would welcome it,
Meeting me is its joy.

I am also the dust,
Every day on my way.
I never complain that my road is too narrow,
Nor my strength is so tiny.
As long as I don't do things perfunctory,
Every day is a happy day.

深呼吸

当阳光刺破云层时
云正在深呼吸
于是血脉通往全身
红透了整个天际

当阳光穿越树隙时
叶正在深呼吸
沁入心扉的气息
潇潇洒洒的惬意

当阳光照耀大地时
我正在深呼吸
暖气氤氲全身
穿透每一丝缝隙

Deep breathing

When the sun is piercing the clouds,
The clouds are breathing deeply.
So the blood leads to her whole body,
Red runs through the whole sky.

When the sun travels through the tree gaps,
The leaves are breathing deeply.
The air refreshes the tree trunk,
All is comfortable and satisfying.

When the sun shines on the earth,
I am breathing deeply.
The heat flows through every gap,
Filling me with energy.

风雨兼程

云感冒了
雷打个喷嚏
电闪出高烧
雨泪流满面
风敲着车窗
顺便搭车
我只能一路
风雨兼程

Go forward in rain and wind

The cloud caught a cold:
The thunder sneezes;
The lightning has a high fever;
The wind is asthmatic;
The rain is transparent blood.
At this moment can't wait but go forward,
To get enough medicine to the environment:
She must be resuscitated without delay.

观日落

车过桥，见日落
黄金球，似团火
乌云涌起托着她
好像心里也不舍

桥已过，日亦过
霞光让云层错落
层层叠叠的山脉
展示非凡的磅礴

太阳已在哪儿躲
神笔将天空描摹
五彩斑斓的天河
流淌着画的轮廓

View the sunset

I see the sunset when I cross the bridge,
A golden ball likes a roll of fire.
Red clouds rise to hold her up,
As if they don't want to let her leave.

The sun is out of sight after the bridge has passed,
The clouds scatter the sunshine.
Then the sky grows darker,
As if the sun is looking for a place to hide.

Where is the sun already hiding?
It is exactly what I want to know.
When I haven't found the answer yet,
A new sun rises again in the east.

落日景象

晚霞
把历史的风景
遗落在街头
晚风
将拾遗的事情
急急地补救
我正寻找落日
却见在山谷里
漫不经心地走

The sunset scene

The Sunset takes the scenery of history left in the street;
The night wind is in a hurry to remedy unfinished things.
I am looking for the thing I just missed.
Oh, a nosegay of love that picked up during the day.

河里的云

河里的云
比天上的云
显得更厚实
天上的云
被蓝天映衬着
像翻飞的白鸽
河里的云
被涟漪浸泡着
像绽放的雪莲

天上的云
总是跃跃欲试
坠落的快感
河里的云
则为向上升腾
而跃跃欲试

Clouds in the river

Clouds in the river,
Whiter than in the sky.
The darker color in the river,
Sets off their brighter.

Clouds in the river,
More thick and solid than in the sky.
They are much more watery;
They can carry much heavier weight.

Clouds in the river,
More mischievous than in the sky.
Ducks bring their food;
The water waves smile at them.

Clouds in the river,
More Industrious than in the sky.
The clouds in the sky always fall down;
The clouds in the river are evaporating constantly.

夏日里的风

夏日里的风
冬日里的梦
醉醺醺的
在这里相逢

我不知什么
是凉的爽
　寒的冻
只觉举轻若重

夏日里的风
飒飒响着
将竹林吹动
他不屑
春的温柔
秋的冷峻
只与冬争雄

汗吹成了雪

雪吹成了汗
才是真的武功
千里燃火
万里冰封
让太阳动容

The wind in summer

In winter dreams,

The summer wind often occurs.

Like a drunk god,

Breaking up the ice and melting it.

Pour into the river;

Pour into the ocean.

Everything is cheering;

The sun is also moved.

My body is getting warm and sweaty,

Leading the impulse in the heart.

Until the autumn girl says: "Hello".

I feel like I haven't woken up yet.

Suddenly there comes another gust of wind,

And immediately turns sweat into snow.

But I know that the summer wind always comes out.

Greeted by the beautiful spring girl.

天空的色彩

天空是蔚蓝的
时间也在深呼吸
每一分每一秒
都在前赴后继
真担心他累着
也该让他歇息

天空是灰色的
时间失去了
阳光的闪熠
让我很难判断
大自然对我
真情还是假意

天空是漆黑的
时间也去了梦里
我对这样的景色
分外地着迷
心也随之奔驰
失去仅存的睡意

The colors of the sky

When the sky is blue,

Time is taking deep breaths.

Every second goes one after another,

We ought to do things quickly.

When the sky is gray,

Time has lost its luster.

It's good for judgement,

Testing if feelings are true or false.

When the sky is black,

Time goes to sleep.

We need to dream quickly,

And make our dreams come true before dawn.

When the sky is pink,

Time is waking up.

We have to get up earlier,

To catch the opportunity renewed.

光与影

渐渐地发现
光所爱的
好像不是你
而是你的影

他把你的影
打扮那么美丽
颀长而离奇
朦胧而清晰

光和影的关系
让你隐隐生气
光和影的亲密
让你深深妒忌

你远远躲避
冷清而孤寂
忧郁而叹息
恍惚而迷离

你已不是
原来的你
头发已斑白
人也上了年纪

你怨他跑得太急
为何日行万里
他说怪不得他
那是身不由己

你想甩开影子
决意离他而去
他挽住你的臂
说他爱的是你

影在一旁嘻笑
我和你本是一体
你恍然大悟
顿觉心旷神怡

夕阳西下
光搂着你
你和他比以往
更加亲密

Light and shadow

I gradually found out,
Whom the light loves.
It must not be you,
But certainly, your shadow.

She's dressed up your shadow,
More beautiful than you are.
Their intimacy between them,
The warmth is like glue.

Not because you are too old,
But for she runs too fast.
If you can catch up with her speed,
Time will slip backwards,
Then you become young.

赞黑洞²⁴照

三年前第一次
见到你的神采
我以为那是
太阳的指环
日光将底色
聚在你的洞口
耀出最灿烂的瞬间

今天再度与你见面
你成了佳人的手环
橘红色的光圈
看起来有些虚幻
三颗璀璨的钻石
是那样的耀眼

24　黑洞（black hole）是爱因斯坦广义相对论预言存在的一种天体。黑洞直接成像确认了黑洞的存在，同时也通过模拟观测数据对爱因斯坦的广义相对论做出了验证。

原来那是挂在
你脖颈上的项链
抑或是套在
你腰间的游泳圈
虽不见你的形态
却略知你的情怀

在宇宙的星辰大海
你时而像孩子一般
荡漾在细波微澜
时而像勇士一般
在星球的塌缩中
飞旋出黑色的世界

Images of the cosmic black hole

First time I saw you,
I thought you were the ring of the sun.
In the most brilliant moment,
I saw the light running through the hole.

The second time I saw you was three years later.
You had become a beautiful bracelet;
Orange aperture with three diamonds
So Bright and dazzling.

New black hole images continuously updated.
Contain clues to cosmic mysteries humans are exploring.
In the sea of stars in the universe.
You look like a child, ever learning.

奇　观

宇航员太空漫步
奇观景象一幕幕
地球在身边飘过
无依无靠的孤独

心头升起的悬念
不知是云还是雾
但她的无比惊艳
将心紧紧地吸住

太空瑰丽的色彩
闪现出大片一部
那是海里的鲸鱼
还是山上的猛虎

人飘逸着却串起
天马行空的思路
大家手拉着手儿
与星星一起跳舞

The wonder of the space

When Taikonaut walked in space,

A midst a stream of scenes spectacular.

The earth lonely drifted by,

And we forgot the moon was even there.

The magnificent red of the sun,

Only shows half her face.

Maybe on meeting a human being,

She became a Little shy.

The stars are having a dance party,

Clearly, to see who is warm and who is cold.

The most honest one is the comet,

With a broom ready for the cleaning.

太空行

宇航员出舱太空行
我随镜头看风景
地球成了背景墙
四周漫漫成舞厅

背景墙悠悠地旋转
美得让人窒息
宇航员翻飞的英姿
酷得让人震惊。

卫星上跳个迪斯科
历史上留下深深脚印
星球磅礴走泥丸
宇宙浩渺任尽兴。

Space walk

Taikonaut steps out into space;
The earth became a background wall.
Space became his huge stage;
No one can match him.

Some said he is dancing disco;
Some said he is playing Tai Chi.
Whatever the action Taikonaut did,
All are records in history.

I seem forgotten I am still on the earth,
Floating into space freely.
I want to dance the Tango with him,
To celebrate his great success.

"祝融号"²⁵的飞抵

大约每隔半个世纪
便有火星陨石飞抵
千百年来生生不息
像派信使那么神秘。

地球人也分外珍惜
将陨石当宝贝藏匿
制作标本切割晶体
捕捉其中每条信息。

我并不懂内在肌理
只见表面五彩闪熠
将我带入童年梦幻
有似曾相识的熟悉。

我手持小小万花筒
在摇曳中闪烁惊异

25　祝融号，为天问一号任务火星车。高度1.85米，重量约240公斤。天问一号任务的科学目标是研究火星形貌与地质构造特征。

彩玻组成瑰丽世界
变幻莫测尽显神奇。

火星给地球的大礼
似我万花筒的记忆
那是火星的万花筒？
是宇宙摇曳的奇迹？

火星地球心心相惜
有天荒地老般创意
一手牵着童年趣事
一手摇拽未来欣喜！

当我还憧憬在梦里
中国火星车已飞抵。
它的名字象征火神
愿将火种撒向星际。

它身披灿烂的虹霓
行走在滚滚的沙砾；
它像彩蝶飞进窗口，
将遥远的美好传递。

它才是地球的使者
穿梭于浩渺的天际。
看星球磅礴走泥丸
是怎样的恢宏大气。

它的神速让人惊奇
似人类想象的瞬移，
它的使命更为神圣
探索外星生命秘密。

Zhu Rong's new mission

The God of Fire, Zhu Rong in Chinese legend,
Believed to live in the Bright Place of Kunlun Mountain.
It is said that he sent the kindling from heaven,
Taught human beings how to use fire.

Now he has given a new task,
To go to and land on Mars.
Like taking a new kindling of fire,
Igniting the hope of inter-planetary exploration.

I once heard Martian meteorites arrived on earth
Every half a century.
But no material from Earth has ever been to Mars,
It's so unfair to the Earth.

Being a messenger mysterious,
The God of Fire Zhu Rong went to the fire star.
The mission was called Tianwen;
Certainly he would ask many questions of the universe.

I also ignited a fire in my dream,

Of driving a space-vehicle into the immense universe.

Humanity's adventure is unending,

Urging me to keep pursuing self-transcendence.

光的形状[26]

光的形状
是穿透黑暗的利剑
让历经沧桑的山河
有神采奕奕的模样

光的形状
是腾云驾雾的魔杖
驱散阴霾
有势不可挡的力量

光的形状
是天穿地裹的霓裳
你有时竟忘了她
她却时刻陪你身旁

光的形状
像亲人般和蔼慈祥
挽起你稚嫩的臂膀
温润你孤独的心房

26　此诗（中英文）发表在《上海外滩》2023 年第 12 期。

光的形状
给人以爱情的力量
她与影的亲密
正在超越地老天荒

光的形状
时而扑朔迷离
那探索世界的目光
在日月星辰轨道上

光的形状
时而一泻千里
穿行于银河的波光
掀起大海奔腾激荡

光的形状
是一刻不停的步伐
她以神秘的速度
总在整个宇宙徜徉

光的形状
无止境地探索密码
连丝丝缕缕尘埃
都揽在她怀里飞扬

The shape of light

The shape of light,
Is a sword through the darkness.
Make vicissitudes mountains and rivers,
Revive to good spirits.

The shape of light,
Is a magic wand.
Dispel the haze,
With unstoppable force.

The shape of light,
Is the neon wardrobe of heaven.
Sometimes you forget about her,
She's always always there for you.

The shape of light,
Is family member's kindness.
Take up your young arms,
Warm your lonely heart.

The shape of light,

Is the irresistible power of love.

Her intimacy with the shadow,

Going beyond the end of time.

The shape of light,

Is a mysterious speed.

Wandering in the whole universe,

At a non-stop pace

The shape of light,

Is the key endlessly reading the password of life.

Through the Milky Way,

And all the tiny sand.

遐 想

时间正下着雨
银河般飘落
我用心点燃
一轮红日喷薄

期待空间折叠
粒子重组
实现三维
向四维的飞跃

我在时光隧道
来回穿梭
星际旅行的阻拦
何以冲破

Reverie

When it was raining hard,

My heart was on fire.

A red sun rises in the Milky Way.

Space now is folding;

Particles now are reorganizing.

I'm now three dimensions around,

Trying to fly into the fourth dimension.

Going into the time tunnel,

Shuttle back and forth.

How I want to fly to the universe,

Take a trip to Mars and Uranus.

第四辑 阅读之魅
The charm of Reading

一袋烟

从活蹦乱跳童年
到步履蹒跚老年
在宇宙的视野里
或许也就一袋烟

时间将生命点燃
生命让时间尽燃
深邃是艺术灵魂
就在永恒的瞬间

Short time and eternal

From lively childhood,

To the staggering steps of old age,

In the view of the universe,

Short as smoking a cigarette.

Time ignites life;

Life burns out time;

Time ignites life makes all times burn out.

What settles down is called the art,

Where the eternal soul is placed,

No one can see through her.

零 拷

日子是零拷[27]的
岁月才是集装箱
老师一声招呼
回到童年时光

慢生活的时代
什么都是散装
柴米油盐酱醋茶
人们抿着嘴说香

快节奏的生活
什么都集装
越大包装越便宜
山姆会员好时尚

光阴已经打包
时间准备罐装
零拷已进博物馆
在人们心中雪藏

---

27 零拷，沪语拆分零售的意思。

Retail and wholesale

Retail is daily;

Wholesale is life.

All past days are retail,

Like the voice of kindergarten;

Tasted very sweet.

Today's day are wholesale,

Like the coming advertise,

Seems fashionable.

The retail days have been packed;

Put in the museum.

The artists go to museums,

Looking at adverts for inspiration for wholesale.

I'd like to retail my days,

And in the future wholesale all of them.

家乡的美

你写尽家乡的美
梯田拥簇山和水
白墙黛瓦的村子
炊烟欲将彩云追

你写尽春天的美
映山红撩人心醉
蜜蜂扇起了天翼
鸟儿歌声更清脆

你写尽心灵的美
恰似窗户的明媚
旌旗卷过的岭上
走过英雄一辈辈

你写尽情丝的美
漫天的花瓣纷飞
烟雨朦胧掩隐你
絲絲缕缕透心扉

You write all the beauty

You write all the beauty of your hometown,
Terraced fields cluster with mountains and water.
Village with white walls and black tiles,
Cooking smoke wants to chase after colorful clouds.

You write all the beauty of spring,
The red of azaleas is tantalizing;
The bees fan up wings in the sky;
The songs of birds are more clearly.

You write all the beauty of your heart,
Just like a bright window.
On the ridge sweeping the banner,
Coming generations of heroes.

You write all the beauty of your love,
The petals fly all over the sky.
The misty rain hides you,
Like a feeling of the heart.

时间的原型

时间被打断骨架
依然连着筋
岁月被磨成碎片
依然留着影

你拾起碎片
修补时间的脉络
让阳光穿透雾霾
照见历史的原型

曾经是璀璨的星
亦闪出云层掩隐
曾经是炽热的情
再点燃红烛的芯

斑驳的篱墙
如褶皱的光阴
撒落在时光隧道
溢满动人的温馨

The noble character of time

Time once interrupted her skeleton,
Cracked her continuity.
Time once pulverized into pieces,
Not to be cherished.

But someone is still yelling,
"Time is life, Time is money!"
And someone is still complaining,
Too busy to have time.

Must mend the skeleton of time;
Must retrieve all the timepieces.
Let time restore its noble character,
Make the life shine more brightly.

天山雪

天山雪飘逸着陆
她有着天父地母
你却从小失去了
父母至亲的呵护

当你从繁华魔都
来到广袤的山麓
天山雪滋润着你
心灵纯洁地复苏

沙漠迷失的遭遇
历练了你的筋骨
逆风而翔的羽翼
冲破了重重险阻

此刻你是天山雪
纷纷扬扬地飞舞
在生命的时光里
剔透得晶莹夺目

Snowflake from Tianshan Mount

Once the snowflake from the Tianshan Mount landed,
On the ground of the Gobi desert barren and desolate.
She lost her parental care when she was young,
Sucked by the yellow sand and no place to go.

Nowadays she falls on the green leaves,
The Gobi now become a large meadow land.
Green leaves embraced her earnestly,
Melting her into its own body gently.

She became steam under the sun,
Flies back into the sky to be snow again.
She feels that she had a permanent life,
Living on the Tianshan Moun even more beautiful!

泪 雨

雨下得淅淅沥沥
泪水比雨水更密集
你想把他即刻拉黑
他却缠绕在你心里

夜倒是比你性急
瞬间拉黑了天地
让时间的雷霆滚过
寂静整理你的回忆

曾经的恋情已逝
曾经的炽烈已熄
春风抽干心中冰雪
屋檐下停了那雨滴

Tears rain

It was falling rain.
Tears are stronger.
You want to block him right now.
He's stuck in your heart.

Night is more urgent than you are,
Instantly blocked the heaven and earth.
Have the thunder of time roll over,
Be quiet to arrange your memory.

The old relationship is gone,
Once the fire died,
The breeze drained the ice in your heart;
Let the rain drops stop.

文学的季风

卷首语像一团火
撩拨着我的心窝
曾经的梦想升起
犹如太阳的喷薄

文学的季风吹过
思南幽静的廊廓
家的温馨在这里
氤氲着书香之墨

岁月打开百宝箱
雪藏珍珠的散落
光阴越出时间舱
梳理生命的执着

天上的星星追着
地上的泰斗闪烁
诗文舒展着双翼
飞向大海的辽阔

The monsoon of literature

The preface is like a fire,

Lighting up my heart.

The first chapter begins with a dream;

Third chapter builds up to a rousing climax.

Magic stories happen one after another,

The epic last to no end.

Readers are reluctant to close their books.

Who blew in the literary monsoon?

Set off countless passionate dreams.

Who could build a huge library?

To store all the wonderful passion.

都市的春播

你是都市的春播
时尚得让人入魔
种子在大地深处
胚胎已成功落座

你是书海的春播
像潮水一般涌过
页码翻卷着雪浪
溢起最美的笑涡

你是文脉的春播
亦犁过多少长河
终以虔诚与智慧
让历史未来胶着

你是心灵的春播
出神入化的魂魄
在每一扇窗户里
都有星光的闪烁

Spring sowing in the city

The center of metropolitan city has no agriculture,
But there still has a spring sowing.
New seeds are fine books;
The field is the heart of the young man.

The seeds will sprout and grow up,
To become a seedling of thought.
Eventually they will become big trees;
The strong backbone of the young.

The seeds sown in the spring;
Are the hope of the harvest.
I am going to be a sowing machine,
Running at a high speed every day.

又见平遥

你用大师的镜头
与平遥古城对话
就像与神对话
一样虔诚肃然

山一样的城门
扛着一爿天
不屈的脊梁
巍峨而庄严

高墙深院
在城池蜿蜒
翘角飞檐
尽显古韵神采

绵延的屋顶
像闪烁的鳞片
倾斜不倒的大树
将寓意深含

你让雕梁画栋
载着千年的风采
你让屋檐艺术
藏着万象的精湛

古城老街的魅力
随大片扑面而来
任凭时光老去
她在那里等待

如诗如画的佳作
闪着快门的瞬间
却是穿越古今
向我款款走来

Seeing Pingyao again

Talking to the ancient town of Pingyao,[28]

Is like a dialogue with God.

Mountain-like gates,

Bear half of the sky.

Unyielding city backbone,

Tall and solemn above the ground.

Carved beams and painted rafters,

Bear the elegant demeanor of old times,

The extension of the eaves,

Like scintillating fish scales.

Once pressed, the camera shutter,

Travels a thousand years to this day.

---

28 Pingyao, a county in the middle of Shanxi province.

思南²⁹风情

这是一部摄影大片
光的璀璨
　　海的气派
这是一部精湛之作
心的呼吸
　　情的释怀

画面伫立着背影
老人 少女 小孩
建筑 小景 物件
其实整个思南
都是历史的背影
却又照进现在
像模特一样
走着时尚的T台

春暖花开的时节

29　指上海市思南路。该路原称马斯南路，系1914年法租界工董局为纪念在1912年8月13日去世的法国著名音乐家 Massenet 而筑。

最浪漫的诗人
变得深邃可爱
像神马穿过浮云
如意象深藏思辨
又一起归于自然

地球村的一角
尽显五彩斑斓
老外像回家般自在
不管是在咖啡店
还是坐在路边
抑或上台出演

黄昏的天地柔和
像光与影的抒怀
悠悠而上的台阶
裸露得温情脉脉
我也曾在这里
留下最美瞬间
像夕阳的余晖
庄重却又灿烂

The feelings of Sinan Road[30]

Exquisite and beautiful villa,

The idea of the master reflected everywhere.

The Shanghai style differs in the details;

The pouring tide is surging toward you.

Every visitor enjoys heartily.

The charm of Sinan Road and the missing south

The cross Fuxing road remind you,

Work hard For the great revival of the nation.

---

30 Sinan Road (思南路), formerly Massenet Rue, was built by the French
Concession Authority in 1914..

七言《思南风情》
——译者和诗

美墅雕琢巨制功
上海气派如潮涌
市民尽享思南美
奋力勇追复兴梦

高耸的衣架

濮院[31]是心中的密码
在采访时邂逅过她
那产销毛衫的女皇
商战中的一枝奇葩

你真用摄影机编出
一套古镇霓裳神话
河流是天然原料场
桥像网机织着彩霞

旋转的涟漪如金梭
粼粼的波光似银发
古老的木屋打开窗
迎接最时尚的升华

福善塔是高耸衣架
小月挂在她的肩下
风衣披上她的身时
云朵亦忙着去绣花

---

31 浙江省濮院镇，浙江省嘉兴市桐乡市一个古镇，地处长江三角洲平原腹地，沪、杭、苏中间节点位置，是全国最大的羊毛衫集散中心。2018 年 5 月，荣登中国最美特色小镇 50 强榜首。

High coat hanger

Puyuan[32] has a secret password in the heart,
Can she open the door of riches while keeping her beauty.
Rivers are natural raw material farms;
The bridge is like a net machine weaving the rosy clouds.
The Fushan Tower is a high coat hanger;
The Moon hung under her shoulder.
When the windbreaker is put on her,
The clouds are busy embroidering.
Around this biggest coat hanger:
The largest sweater market in China.

32　Puyuan（濮院）, an ancient town in Tongxiang, Jiaxing, Zhejiang province.

致文友

你是闪电
劈开了历史的瞬间
让人回眸窥探。
你是雨点
连成了一条长河
让人流连忘返。
你是雷声
于无声处响起
炸出一池狂澜。
你是风暴
在灵魂深处席卷
让心翻江倒海。

月亮悄悄地
从屋后爬上来
偷窥你的
读史百篇。
灯光慢慢地
从屋子退出来

招呼晨曦

为你庆典。

朝霞悠悠地

甩起水袖五彩

风姿绰约

无比惊艳。

小草羞羞地

含着露珠

晶莹璀璨

灵动万千。

太阳嘻嘻地笑着

像个老小孩

夸奖你的卓越

表达他的礼赞

To literary friend

You are the lightning,

Splitting the moment of history.

You are the rain drop,

Gathering into a big river.

You are the thunder,

Exploding the silence.

You are the storm,

Sweeping the depths of the soul.

Oh, you are only my friend:

The bright moon in my night.

等 你

我在渡口等你
你载我去哪里
上下五千年
纵横千万里。

船舱里有你
读史的笔记
洋洋洒洒肆意
像耕耘的田地。

我猛地回头看
已过半个世纪
那时你还年轻
正开着拖拉机。

黑黢黢的土地
银闪闪的大犁
你犁出的竟是
你人生的轨迹。

Wait for you

You were young at that time,
Drove a tractor in the rice field.
I stood at the end of the field,
Waiting to give you thanks and food.

Half a century has passed but you are still young,
Using a computer in the literature field.
I'm standing in the middle of the field,
Waiting to read your new book.

You plow in all the fields you pass through,
Because you are a big golden plough yourself.
I'm standing at the side of your field,
Waiting to see the trajectory of your life.

赞 "微冲"

"微冲" [33]
有多神勇
我不懂
我只见他的笔
蘸着一波波
大潮涌动
从他笔尖
喷出的火力
就是 "微冲"

微冲的点射
一枪命中
微冲的连发
无比威猛

于是他的笔
点射——
细节剪出的窗花

___
33　微型冲锋枪的简称。

贴上心灵的窗户
美若女神
连发——
向着历史的天空
绽放出礼花
万紫千红

Praise "the mini-weapon"

The worker must have a tool;
The farmer must have a plow;
The warrior must have a gun;
He must have a mystery weapon.

He calls his item as a "mini-assault rifle",
Formerly a pen but now a computer.
Words are the daily bullets he fires
Paper and screens are his battlefield

Every word bullet can hit its target;
He is waving the flag on the field of honour.
He wins one battle after another
One heart after another.

爱的心房

新婚之夜
他离开了她
入侵者将战火
燃到他的家乡

他抱着机枪
犹如抱着
他的新娘
用灼热的脸
贴着冰冷的钢

滚烫的枪膛
是爱的心房
喷出的火舌
是滚滚的岩浆

天空飘过一朵云
他看见她的泪行
树间投下一道亮

他看见她的泪光

思念的雨滴
在天上架起彩虹
像鹊桥一样
渺茫　幻象
但愿能缚住苍龙
还他安宁的家乡

Heart of love

On wedding Night,
Farewell to the bride.
The invaders were coming,
A shotgun must be carried.

Hatred of the enemy,
Exploded in the barrel of the gun.
The love of beloved,
Passed between the front line and the rear.

There is the expectation of the bride that
life will be strong.
Family members are waiting:
Victory will be in the front.

快 递

年轻人的恋爱
还真有点神秘
虽然彼此倾心
却不说我爱你

那天放学时分
他急急告诉她
门口有她快递
让她好顿寻觅

见他远远走来
像上舞台演戏
略施一些装扮
帽子压得很低

她正感觉好奇
问他什么用意
"我已把自己
快递给了你！"

Express delivery

The love of young, now-abandoned old tunes:
"I love you more than I can say!"
"I can't imagine life without you!"
No longer say such words today.

One day when work was over,
The girl in love received a notice:
"There is an express delivery package with the doorman,
Go and get it without delay."

The girl asked who sent the delivery.
The doorman told a name that excited her:
Exactly was the boyfriend in her love,
She is waiting for something right now.

She was guessing what item was delivered.
Cosmetics, little toys, or a food she likes?
She even thought of bras and underwear,
Suddenly her face turned red.

She hurried to the doorman,

Saw a young man standing upright,

Wearing a white suit.

Doorman said the express delivery was the boy.

"The white suit is the express delivery package,

Inside the package is my body.

I deliver all myself to you,

Including my heart, my love and my whole life."

The girl was deeply moved and burst into tears,

Exactly what she had expected for many days.

She sent an express delivery back immediately,

Throwing her whole body into the boy's arms.

尾声——光阴似箭[34]

光阴似箭
射穿了多少洞隙
时间如水
在洞隙悄悄流过
我担心时间的枯竭
生命的长河
会不会走向沙漠

光阴似箭
在日日夜夜穿过
时间如云
在浩渺天空漂泊
风吹起她的银发
我担心她的老去
不再将雨滴洒落

光阴似箭
将冬的寒霜击落

---

34 此诗（中英文）发表在《上海外滩》2023 年第 8 期封二。

时间如梭
编织着银缎被窝
雪花飘入
我的脑沟深壑
将我的灵感激活

光阴似箭
穿越了岁月蹉跎
时间如涡
旋转出天高地阔
让我不再疑惑
用夕阳的那把火
点燃人生的余热

光阴似箭
惊扰了尘埃王国
时间如环
让箭插上了心窝
生命犹如瞬移
弹指一挥间探索
飞向遥远的星座

Time's like an arrow

Time's like an arrow,
Piercing countless holes.
My life's like water quietly seeping through the holes.
I worry that the time will be exhausted.
The long river of life will flow to the desert.

Time's like an arrow,
Through the day and night.
My life's like a cloud wandering in the vast sky.
I worry that it will be older,
No more raindrops will fall.

Time's like an arrow,
Shooting down the frost of winter.
My life's like a shuttle weaving a white satin quilt,
The snowflakes drifted into my brain,
Activating my inspiration with silver hair.

Time's like an arrow,

Going through wasted days.

My life's like a vortex spinning out of the stratosphere,

Making me hesitate no longer,

Igniting the rest of my life with the fire of the setting sun.

Time's like an arrow,

 Frightening the earthly realm.

My life's like a target guiding the arrow into the heartm

A transient voyage of discovery,

Flying to an ever-distant constellation.

关于诗的对话（代后记）
Postscript: A dialogue about poetry

诗译者丁海椒（下简称"译"）:《霜雨集》经过整理和翻译，终于要问梓了。您一定有许多感想要对读者说吧？

诗作者王雅萍（下简称"作"）：出一本诗集是我曾经的梦想，后来被友人的一番忠告击得粉碎，"你还是写你的小说吧，尽管是业余作家，毕竟也获得过文学的奖项，也拥有一个读者群。写小说可以凭借你的想象虚构人物情节，凭借一定的篇幅，遮挡掉你写作的很多弱点。读者有时被人物打动或被情节吸引，对你写得不到位的地方也就忽略不计了。而诗集，那是一目了然的清晰，把你所有的毛病都裸露在外，躲都没法躲，藏都没法藏的。"忠言逆耳，却深邃得直抵人心。从此，我将这个梦想藏入心底。当然友人为我关上了一扇门，也给我打开了一扇窗，"你可以将自己感觉还不错的诗，一首一首地发在网上或刊物，这样效果可能更好。"那次我在网上发了一首小诗《母亲河》，不仅得到网友的点赞，更让我意外的是你把我的《母亲河》译成了英文。外语是我们这代人的弱项，我想都不敢想。凭着是自己写的诗，我看懂了你译文的意思。译得真好！心里涌起一阵波澜，那个梦又悄悄地浮出水面。

译：那次翻译你的《母亲河》，也是被诗感染，一时冲动之作。

作：不久后你给我发来为著名作家张嵩山老师翻译的诗，原诗是这样的：

> 不用踮起脚跟，
> 就能望见那最后的桥，
> 模样不太真切，
> 应该像家乡的青石，
> 拱曲在母亲淘米的河上。

译文是：

> Don't have to stand on your toes,
> You can see the last bridge.
> It doesn't look very real.
> Should be like home Bluestone,
> Arched over the river which Mother used to wash rice.

这样的诗既像临摹了一幅画，又给你带来无限想象，更蕴含着深邃的哲理。我的心也再次点燃了。

译：张嵩山是我在部队时的战友，共事多年，也互相切磋。这首诗也是一时冲动译的，结果他还很满意。需要说明的是，我的英语可不是科班出身，自己学的，谬误肯定有不少。翻译诗是见笑了。不过我胆子大，不怕交流。退休前因公出国，也是不带翻译的。所以斗胆去翻译诗。在这个过程中，会比较不同语言的诗。我看到你诗的时候，会想起美国现代诗人埃米莉·狄金森（Emily Dickinson）。她也是女性，在世时只发表了很少量的诗，但去世后却声名大作，被称为美国现代诗的开拓者。

作：对，你给我介绍过她，并把她的一首知名小诗连同你自己做的中文翻译发给了我：

I'm nobody! I'm nobody!

Who are you?

Are you nobody, too?

Then there's a pair of us--don't tell!

They'd banishi us, you know!

How dreary to be somebody!

How public, like a frog,

To tell your name the livelong day,

To an admiring bog!

我是无名之辈，你是谁？

你也是无名之辈？

咱俩可真是一对，

别告诉谁，·

他们会把咱们挤兑！

当个名人多烦恼，

像只青蛙哇哇乱叫

整天炫耀自己的名号，

陷入不可自拔的泥淖！

译：这首诗之所以会流行，我觉得是它触发了人心里微妙之处，引发了心理共鸣。这是女性诗人的细腻和特长。我觉得你的许多诗有这个味道。

作：你说我的诗有许多方面与她很相像。这句话就像在我心里撒了把火星，将我的梦想点燃。只是我依然少量地一首一首地发着自己的诗。

译：今天你要多谈一点你诗的想法。

作：我对诗歌一直处于似懂非懂的状态，哪有什么自己的看法与观点。只是因为喜欢，总拿着笔在那里涂鸦，到底涂成了什么，自己也说不出来。

译：作诗不是写理论。写理论要彻底、清晰。作诗有时真是要保持点朦胧。

作：我对自己涂出来的东西并不满意，总是奢望能涂出更理想的东西。什么才是理想的诗呢？我终于在专家的评论中找到了答案：创新文体——提供不可预测的联想——新颖、无法解释的逻辑——改变对诗的认知——创造完全陌生的语境，逃避释义，从而打破原有思维，改变处理现实的能力，扩大了对世界的想象力……我对照着自己看到过的那些理想的诗，那真是有这样的大气和魄力。那是需要诗人的灵感、灵气和灵性，才能写出那样灵动的诗。这下我不再懵懂，我完全明白了理想的诗在文学殿堂里的位置，那是皇冠顶上的明珠，可望而不可即。从此再也不梦想自己能写出什么理想的诗。自己已年逾古稀，在社会上，已被称为"老小孩"，我还是像小孩那样去涂鸦吧，尽兴而已。也不再羞于将自己的拙作拿出来给人看，就让那些涂鸦像一片片秋叶那样飘落，五彩缤纷的样子，让人们在上面"咔嚓咔嚓"地走，留下生活的情调与惬意，足矣！

译：你说得很有趣。我年轻时候也写过一点诗，也有过类似的想法。不过后来因工作责任重而放弃了。

作：你年轻时曾被选为空军诗人，作品收入空军诗集。我给你发了《我的影子》后，你即刻为我和了一首。我觉得你的中文诗写得很棒的，是我喜欢的那款。

译：过奖了。这些年，我的著述还是更多地聚焦在评论（含杂文）和理论，以及我退休后去大学带 MPA 研究生项目上。有话说，"理论是灰色的，生命之树常青。"我蓦然看到你仍在生命之树之下，生发出新鲜的枝叶，这正是我应该学习的。

作：我写了一首《光阴似箭》，以一位古稀之人的眼光去审视、去担忧、去抒发自己的情怀。你将它一节一节地翻译出来，让我感动不已。

译：当然，如果译诗，翻译者自己是否写过诗，是否能理解诗是不同的。译诗，是在两种不同的语言，两种不同的文化之间穿梭。中文与英文在诗的方面，有不同的格式和要求，但在诗意方面，却往往是相通、相容，甚至是相同的。所以我想采用意译的方法，不拘泥于文字的语句对应，着眼于把诗的意境挖掘出来，加以凝练、拓展、发挥，甚至在自己也产生诗兴的时候，加以新的创意。我把这种翻译方法叫做"创意译"。"创意译"使得我更敢于放开手脚，也因此生发了我的几首和诗。我很感谢你对此的理解和宽容，还不断给我鼓励。

作："创意译"好，这增色了我的作品。你重视在翻译过程中把握诗的意境。在翻译过程中，你特别注重在意境上的提炼，比如《月与雪》，比如《我见过你》，比如《烟雨廊桥》等，让诗的意境在译文中进一步升华。你的"创意译"为《霜雨集》增色不少。《光阴似箭》出来后，我们就投稿《上海外滩》杂志。杂志不仅将这首诗以双语形式刊登于封二，还设计了相配的画面，与诗的意境氛围相合。看不清她是朝阳还是夕阳，只看见她灿烂如火。那种燃烧，既是光阴，也是时间，让人的思绪，在永恒与不永恒之间，徘徊、忐忑，激越、澎湃！

译：这首诗以及译文的发表，给了我更多翻译诗的勇气和动力。于是就有了鼓励你出集子的想法。

作：对呀。这时我的梦想再也藏不住了，像火星一样的飞了出来。你提出建议，让我将平时写的诗整理出来，由你来翻译成英语，出一本集子。我的感觉，这像是梦中的礼花。我整理出近百首诗作，交给你，心里是很忐忑的。自己的这些拙作，实在不值得你去费这么大的心思，花这么大的精力翻译。在我还没太想明白的时候，你已译了几首发给我。我还是凭着对自己写的诗的熟悉，朦朦胧胧地看着译文，感觉特别棒。我特别喜欢这种"创意译"，诗歌讲究的就是意象、意韵、意境，意译当然是最好的。就这样，我读着自己的诗，看着译文，心里突然冒出来一个想法，这是一本双语版的诗集，用"双语"的谐音，这本集子就该叫《霜雨集》了。

译：你提出这个书名后，我说如果采用此名，该有一篇"霜雨诗"。

作：对呀，否则读者怎么理解《霜雨集》呢？你的反应真快！当时，我也很兴奋，如果有"霜雨诗"就可以做这个集子的《序》了！"霜雨诗"怎么写？都是两个很具象的自然现象，也是两个很深邃的诗的意象，怎么想象都可以。只是出现在我眼前的霜，竟然不是地上的霜，而是头上的霜，身上的霜。那是我下乡北大荒当知青时，每年秋收，都得早出晚归。北方的这个季节，早晚已经很凉了，而一干活，头上、身上冒出来的热气，遭遇大自然的凉气，于是头发上，即刻挂满霜花，背上也出现一片片白花花的霜；我想象中的雨，也不是从天上落下来的，而是心里时常飘起的心雨……就在我还沉浸在深深的回忆之时，你已发过来你的霜雨诗了："秋天有两种语言／一个是雨／一个是霜。"一句话，就将"双语"和"霜雨"都定义好了！整首诗紧紧贴着大自然的四季风情展开，最后落到大地母亲的情怀，"她会将霜和雨全数收集／去迎接来年必到的春光！"整首诗将《霜雨集》诠释得既大气，又细腻，所有的想象和曼妙都蕴含在其中。是《霜雨集》最贴切的《序》了。

译：我要感谢你接受这个《序》。我曾经给我的几位朋友的著作写过序。但用诗作序还是第一次。

作：还有，这个集子的书名《霜雨集》的翻译，你翻译成"The Sound of Frost and Rain"（霜和雨的声音），既有诗意，又对应了序诗中的"好在有大地慈祥的母亲，容得下各种不同的声响"这样有思想内涵的语句。

译：自然界的霜本来是没有声音的，淅沥沥的雨，声音也不算大。用霜和雨的"声音"作题，会引起读者的联想。

作：这本书的注释，基本都是你做的，你怎么考虑这个问题，介绍一下好吗？

译：一些地方做些注释是必要的。因为读者对象不同，需要用注释来说明。比方说，"零拷"这个沪语词汇，不作

272

解释其他地方人可能不了解，但英译里已经翻译成"Retail"，所以英文注释不必了。还有些地名，如果从诗文或译文没有明确写明的，就做个注释，反之就不做了。此外，有的诗文和译文已经刊物上发表过，也加以注明，以表示对刊物及其编辑的感谢。

作：在翻译《霜雨集》的同时，我听你说还在写一篇哲学论文。

译：是的。我应学界同仁提议，为 2024 年 8 月将在意大利罗马召开的第二十五届世界哲学大会准备一篇哲学论文，我拟的题目是:《老子"道法自然"理念与"消灭战争"观诠释(Lao Zi's Concept of "The Way follows nature" and "War Elimination" View)》。虽然篇幅不需很长，但总有点累而枯燥。搞搞你那些诗歌，正好转换脑子呢。

作：该称你双枪神手啦! 只是，要多多保重! 我曾经告诉你，诗歌翻译可以往后拖拖的!

译：其实，要感谢你给我翻译诗歌的机会，让我可以换换脑子，不至于陷入"盲热"(fever of blind)。诗歌和哲学都是人类精神生产的璀璨之花，它们之间，并不是毫无关系，更不是互相排斥，而是互为衬托、交相辉映。哲学从诗歌中对精彩生活和丰富情感的描绘和抒发中获取养分和灵气，诗歌从对自然界、人类社会一般规律的深邃的哲学思考的启发中得以更深、更集中地切入人们的心灵，化作不竭的精神势能。在《霜雨集》的翻译还没有搞完的时候，哲学论文的初稿就已经完成了，网上提交后不久，就得到消息，大会准备接受这篇论文，要我做些小的修改。我发去中英文两种语言的修改稿后，大会网站一周后就显示"Accepted"(接受）。我的《老子"道法自然"理念与"消灭战争"观诠释》为第二十五届世界哲学大会入选论文。而这个时候，《霜雨集》也正好定稿了。两个作品好像是并蒂花，同时争相开放。

作：是的，祝贺你，也祝贺我们的《霜雨集》。

译：谢谢！说到这里，我要特别感谢一位美国友人David N Henry。他与我同龄，已经在上海生活了30余年了。在译稿完成之后，他花了很多时间予以文字上的校正。（I would also like to express my special thanks to our American friend David N Henry. He is my age and has lived in Shanghai for more than 30 years. He spent a lot of time correcting the text after the translation was finished.）

作：是的。在《霜雨集》即将出版之际，在我的梦想终于成真之时，内心是无比激动的。感谢老小孩网站让我跨过门槛，登上发表诗歌的平台；感谢《上海外滩》杂志为我打开了一扇窗，首次在封二推出双语诗歌，才有了《霜雨集》的创意；感谢黄晔婷老师的牵线搭桥和倾情推介；感谢"浦江思源"的文友对我创作的热忱鼓励，我的诗歌才能走到今天；感谢我的先生是我每首诗歌的第一读者，肯定和否定都有着决定性的意义；感谢同窗好友王雅军的热心点拨；感谢作协臧建民老师的悉心指教；感谢上海文艺出版社接纳了我，让我的诗集有了诞生地；感谢徐如麒、毛静彦老师的精心编辑；感谢孙豫苏、兰伟琴老师的用心设计；感谢刘树昇老师的艺术摄影作品成为诗集的封面。感谢生活的多彩，给我带来创作的灵感；感谢上苍的眷顾，为我派来最好的双语诗歌的指教老师，《霜雨集》是我和海椒老师的共同成果！

礼花已在星空绽放，感谢读者的厚爱！